GOOD OVERCOMES EVIL

The Revival of Goodness as Transforming Power,
and The Return of The Church as The Good Guys

Published by Aventine Press
55 East Emerson St.
Chula Vista CA 91911
www.aventinepress.com

Library of Congress Control Number: 2015915754

ISBN: 978-1-59330-892-6

Printed in the United States of America

GOOD OVERCOMES EVIL

The Revival of Goodness as Transforming Power, and The Return of The Church as The Good Guys

TROY A. BREWER

For Leanna
The good thing I found 26 years ago.
Proverbs 18:22

CONTENTS

INTRODUCTION
Wearing this white hat

I really don't know what causes most people to write books, but I want to tell you why I wrote this one. I also don't know if you have ever been to Highland Park in the north part of Dallas, but it is a hoity-toity kind of place. Lots of brand new facilities and "real old money" in the midst of first class organizations, fine dining, and super shopping.

I am from way south of Ft. Worth, which is the polar opposite of just north of Dallas, but I typically feel very comfortable in all kinds of places. This was the case on that afternoon.

I was sitting at a table with my personal and professional advisor in all things fundraising, Mr. Matt Frazier, and Doug Hudson, a product development guru and really smart guy who runs *Gotothehub.com.*

I was obviously out of my league. There were two really sharp knives in this cerebral drawer of three, but that's ok. I can make good use of really smart people.

I was meeting these guys to get ideas on how to help a much larger audience really grasp the heart of Jesus and see true transformation. *What do I need to put in the hands of people, beyond what I am already doing, that truly gives life and transformation in Christ?*

I'm an author, so we came to the subject of books.

"Troy, I think there are three kinds of books you should write as your next project," Doug said.

"One is something like, *How to reach Christians for Jesus.* I know you're all about that. Another would be along the lines of *How Good overcomes Evil* because it's a huge part of your life message."

I was scribbling in my journal while chewing linguini.

"The third idea is something like your greatest hits, a book on all the stuff you are really into, but divided by chapters."

So I left there, drove through a mess of traffic, and was serious about bringing very real, modern ideas and kingdom born language for these subjects. I decided to take on hell with a water pistol.

Boom!

So that's how this started. Well kinda…

HEROS AND VILLAINS

When I watch a movie, I like it when the good guy is a good guy and the bad guy is a bad guy. I don't like it when all of that is blurred. It's one of the great reasons I am such a fanatic about the *goodness* of God.

None of it is blurred.

There is no evil in the *goodness* of God. There is no evil in God at all. He is good, His intentions and plans are good. What He does is good because that's who He chooses to be and He never changes His mind. Jesus is the most amazing and wonderful person the world has ever seen. He's just plain awesome!!!

But in the church all of that looks like a 3-D movie without the glasses. If the same Spirit that raised Jesus from the dead, that kind of goodness, lives in us, why is the church so obviously messed up?

The problem with America, our families, and our communities has to do with a real deficit of God's *great goodness* in our lives in a way that is real. The problem is not that there aren't enough Christians, the problem is that there's not enough goodness.

When the church is the good guy, it's so powerful. The kingdom of God transforms lives, heaven invades earth, and everything is better.

When the church is the bad guy, it's also so powerful. The mob of hell swallows people whole, hell binds and controls people, and everything is miserable. It doesn't have to be like that.

As a pastor of a large, thriving church and a director of food banks and orphanages I know first hand what happens when you get a real revelation of God's *goodness* and how things change when we become the *good guys*.

Let's you and me talk about that.

Whatever this book is going to be it will not be boring, and whatever results will come from you getting God's goodness into your life, it will not be minimal. I will not promise that this book is good, but I promise this book has Good in it. Let's both dive into it and see what happens.

Troy

CHAPTER I

GOD IS GOOD LOOKING

Putting a true face on the goodness of God

This may come as a shock to you but God is *good.* No, really. God is real and so is His goodness. Ok, I might have just lost a bunch of you, especially a bunch of you Christians.

I think God has gotten the worst P.R. imaginable from His kids, and you and I have not represented His *goodness* very well over the past 2,000 years. Part of that is because I don't think we have really believed God is all that good. In this book, we're going to go for the throat of anything rising against a real, supernatural revelation of how good God really is.

The *goodness* of God is a very foundational principle. It's been under a bunch of dirt for a long time, but it's worth it's weight in gold to do an archeological dig.

God is good and the devil is bad. You can teach a three- year- old this but it's nearly impossible to grasp it after the third year of seminary. No matter how smart you think you are, it's that simple truth that changes everything and makes us free. Our childlike faith in the *goodness* of God causes us to receive the kingdom of heaven, first in salvation and then in our victorious journey through life.

> *"Truly I tell you, anyone who will not receive the kingdom of God like a little child will never enter it."*
>
> –Mark 10:15 NIV

COTTON PATCH

When I was a kid, all of us munchkins would fold our hands, close our eyes, and repeat our memorized prayer in our best country bumpkin accents before every meal.

"God is great, God is good. Let us thank Him for our food..."

When did our prayer life change from, "God I know You're good," to "God I hope You're in a good mood"?

It changed when we grew up and our history of bad became longer than our history of knowing God's goodness. Something happens between our first day of school and our second or third marriage.

After years of just bad, that is, being bad, talking bad, living bad, experiencing bad, and feeling bad we recreate God in our own self image. As our awareness went from bad to worse, our good God died in a frozen plane crash with Buddy Holly and the Big Bopper.

Through the lens of our messed up life we become less convinced that God is really all that good after all.

TRUE LOVE'S KISS

Everybody knows that God is life. We are programmed to connect God with life before we are even born. If our lives are really not that good, then the conclusion of the jury after a brow beating from a demonic Johnny Cochran lawyer is that God is really not all that good after all.

There it is.

Once we bite into that poisoned apple, we become bewitched. It takes a miracle from the Prince of Peace to kiss us with His *goodness* again and awaken us to our righteousness.

> *Awake to righteousness, and do not sin. . . .*
>
> –I Corinthians 15:34

THE WOW FACTOR

The one-two punch of God's *goodness* is the wow factor, or the *glory of God* in our relationship with Him. When we don't see God's goodness, we miss the glory of God.

Moses, the old testament rock star, and marvel comic superhero, who parted the Red Sea and turned the Nile River into blood, wanted a back stage pass to the greatest show on earth. Dissatisfied with the depth of his relationship with God, the way Oliver Twist would be dissatisfied with "three meals of thin gruel a day, an onion twice a week, and half a roll on Sundays." Moses approached the Creator in childlike faith and dared to ask for more.

> *". . .show me your glory."*
>
> –Exodus 33:18

So here in the bible we have this big drama worthy of a Hans Zimmer soundtrack. Maybe one of the all time epic moments in all of history, where God is going to let Moses in on something He doesn't let anybody else in on.

Moses is going to get a peek, a glimpse, a shimmering second or two at the very heart of who God actually is. Not God's works, not God's ways, but Moses is actually going to get to see what God really, really, really looks like.

This is how God answers the brother:

> *And the LORD said, "I will cause all my goodness to pass in front of you, and I will proclaim my name, the LORD, in your presence. . ."*
>
> –Exodus 33:19 NIV

GOODNESS IS WHAT GOD LOOKS LIKE.

You know the Bible gives amazing descriptions of how awesome Jesus is. I mean, He really is the single most amazing person in the universe.

The first and last, the Alpha and Omega
(Rev. 22:13) "Alpha" and "Omega" are the first and last letters of the Greek alphabet (see also Rev. 1:17; Rev. 2:8; Rev. 21:6). This means that He is

described as the beginning of all things articulated and the very end of everything expressed.

His Word is The Light (John 1:1,14) The Bright and Morning Star (Rev. 22:16). He is even the Sun of Righteousness in Malachi 4:2 and the Rising Sun in Luke 1:78. I guess that's why He is described as the true Light in John 1:3-9 and in Isaiah 9:2.

He's The Righteous One in Acts 3:14 and several other places like Jeremiah 23:6; 33:15-16; Acts 7:52 and 22:14.

There are times when Jesus even describes Himself. These are called The "I Am" sayings of John's Gospel. Go ahead and break out your Bible. Let's do a study on how Jesus describes Himself.

Look at this:

"I AM" sayings of Jesus	Bible Verses
I AM	John 8:58
I AM the Bread of Life	John 6:35
I AM the Light of the World	John 8:12; 9:5
I AM the Gate	John 10:7-10
I AM the Good Shepherd	John 10:11-14
I AM the Resurrection and the Life	John 11:25
I AM the Way, the Truth, and the Life	John 14:6
I AM the True Vine	John 15:1-5

I could go on and on, and there have been a lot greater theologians than me that have written well on these subjects throughout the centuries. Obviously, I am skipping a stone across a very large pond, but the point is that these pictures of Jesus are descriptive of His character but not of His appearance.

HIS HOLY MUG SHOT

The biblical pictures of Jesus are descriptions of His titles, His ministry and so on. Never is there a single description that expresses what Jesus looks like in a very relatable, down-to-earth form.

Prophetically, when Isaiah wrote about His form in Isaiah 53:2 he said, "…He has no form or comeliness; And when we see Him, *there is* no beauty that we should desire Him."

You don't find scriptures like this:

> *"And he stoodeth at six foot two with blue eyes and jet blacketh hair. Yea, His countenance was muscular and his skin complexion was olive as iseth common among the Jews."*
>
> –Troy's Bazaar Bogus
> Bible Translation

No, other than supernatural descriptions of the appearance of Jesus, like at the beginning of the book of Revelation, we have no descriptions of how Jesus actually looked in human form.

I am convinced this is completely on purpose. Don't you think that it's odd, that a book having over 31,000 scriptures testifying of the Lord Jesus Christ would not actually describe the human appearance of Jesus?

It doesn't describe the physical appearance of Jesus but actually the Bible does declare exactly what Jesus looks like in human form: *GOODNESS!*

GOODNESS IS WHAT JESUS LOOKS LIKE

I can see Jesus when I see God's goodness. The world can see Jesus when His people demonstrate His heart through goodness.

Since that's the case it's no wonder to me why so much of the world doesn't see Jesus.

Do you really want to know what Jesus looks like? Jesus looks like white and black people standing together with Martin Luther King Jr. against a horrible spirit in a wonderful nation. Jesus looks like a veteran being welcomed home at an airport and honored for his service. Jesus looks like an orphan or a young man being brought into a family after years of not being wanted by anyone. Jesus looks like a helpful visit to a lonely old lady. Sometimes Jesus looks like a bag of groceries or a check to pay somebody's light bill.

I don't know what Jesus physically looked like 2,000 years ago, but I am sure He looked like the thirty-three-year-old descendant of King David that He was. I am also sure that what people saw in Him was not just His Jewish features but they actually saw the heart of the Father.

I know what Jesus looks like. He looks like the heart of the Father. Jesus looks *good*.

God's *goodness* and the face of Jesus are seen on this earth as selfless acts of His people. You see what He looks like in one less victim of abuse, one less addict, one less dropout, and one less suicide. God's *goodness* is seen in one more restoration, one more transformation, one more person walking into something better and higher for their life. As Christians, that's our job.

That's what Jesus looks like and Jesus is exactly what the Father looks like!

> *The Son is the radiance of God's glory and the exact representation of His being...*
>
> –Hebrews 1:3 NIV

Jesus is the exact image of God (see also John 14:9; 2 Corinthians 4:4; Colossians 1:15).

FAINTING GOATS AND SHEEP

When we see heaven invading this planet, when we see the kingdom or the heart of King Jesus or the face of God Himself, we see goodness. If we can keep from twisting off but instead continue until we overcome, it's because we actually see goodness, and through that we know God is real and that He is with us.

> *I had fainted, unless I had believed to see the goodness of the LORD in the land of the living.*
>
> –Psalm 27:13 KJV

Our belief that God is good and that He will do good upon our behalf is the *supernatural seatbelt* that keeps us from falling out.

When you see *goodness,* in any of the forms I just mentioned, or in any form I didn't, you do not see evil. Evil is diminished and downgraded the moment goodness shows up.

MY GOODNESS, GOODNESS IS IMPORTANT!

So are you starting to see it? If we don't see the *goodness* of God, we faint. We fall out. We live our lives with pastor issues and theological problems never to be resolved.

If we don't see the *goodness* of God, we don't see the face, the heart, or the glory of God. If we fail to see goodness we start to fall into unbelief. We have trouble believing God is good after all and that is what sin actually is.

> *But he who doubts is condemned. . .for whatever is not from faith is sin.*
>
> –Romans 14:23

When we sin, we fall short of the Glory of God

> *"for all have sinned and fall short of the glory of God"*
>
> –Romans 3:23

So the problem is not that we don't have enough Bibles. The problem is not that we don't have enough churches. The problem is not that we don't have enough preachers.

What we need is more goodness. We need open displays of God's selfless, giving heart in business, our families, entertainment, politics, and everywhere else in every arena by brave pioneers in undiscovered countries.

I am a hope fanatic because I believe that God is *good* and that God does *good* as David said 3,000 years ago in Psalm 119:68

> *You are good, and do good. . . .*
>
> –Psalm 119:68

I believe that when God's goodness did show up for Moses' mind blowing concert, that God *"abounded in goodness"* as the Bible declares in Exodus 34:6.

God loves to show off His goodness and I think He wishes that we would show off His goodness.

When we look like *Goodness,* we look like Jesus and we become His express image.

Let's you and me try. Let's look like Jesus and demonstrate Jesus through goodness so that we can prove how awesome Jesus really is. People really need to see Him.

Because GOOD OVERCOMES EVIL.

"How far that little candle throws his beams! So shines a good deed in a weary world"
–William Shakespeare, *The Merchant of Venice*

CHAPTER 2

A MILE IN HIS SHOES

The Goodness of God in a Mexican Trash dump

The dump in Matamoros, Mexico was not a nice place to be. It was cartel owned and ruled. People were murdered and enslaved there. Unable to pay off loans, families were rounded up and given quotas to mine for anything of value. It was full of forced labor, human trafficking, and outright slavery. Some people hadn't been allowed to leave the dump in decades. Some were born there and didn't know of a world that was clean and beautiful because they had never lived anywhere else.

In the sixteen years and well over 120 visits I spent doing a work in there, I can tell you that it was the most extreme and hopeless environment I have ever seen anywhere throughout the earth. It was bad and it needed a goodness injection.

So how bad could it be? Well, the heat of the summer made it especially bad. It was full of shrimp and fish guts from huge commercial gulf canneries, green toxic smoke from burning chemicals made the air unbreathable, and it was always burning. Always.

The metro area has the highest population in the state of Tamaulipas with just about a million and half people, and Mexicans don't flush toilet paper. They send it all to the dump.

So you can let your mind imagine how filthy and toxic this environment really was, but you are not going to be able to get there. It was worse than that.

Do not be overcome by evil, but overcome evil with good.

–Romans 12:21

GET OUT OF THE DUMPS

It's easy, actually lazy, to become very impressed with evil and not do anything about it. It wants us to become paralyzed with depression over bad things and never make a move against it.

It knows *good* overcomes evil.

Evil doesn't have to remain. It just takes hard work sometimes, confrontation, courage, commitment, and faithfulness to bring a little bit of good into a majorly dark place. While it might take a lot of effort to bring a little good, it doesn't take a lot of good to overcome a lot of evil. Just a little bit of *good* threatens the entire machine of evil.

> *A little leaven leavens the whole lump.*
>
> –Galatians 5:9

I think that God has called us all to be Holy Ghost gremlins to the mechanics of evil. We should be the lead balloon to evil's parade. We should be the conversation stopper to the noise it likes to speak.

The problem is that we think we have to have the whole thing planned out, when actually, all we have to do introduce goodness.

GOODNESS REDEEMS

So there we were, a team of thirty some odd members from OpenDoor Church. We were feeding people, giving them clean water, new clothes, prayer, and even paying off the debts of families so that we could actually purchase them from the people who owned their debt.
It was a redemptive work in a very real way.

My friends came to me and said, "Pastor Troy, you have to meet this guy." There were hundreds of needy people there, maybe even a thousand, but this guy was special.

GOODNESS IS GREAT

His name was Alexander. He had worked for the Mexican Cartel as a drug runner and low level hit man. The fast cars, nice clothes, and allure for power was a no brainer for a guy that hated being powerless. He had a wife and two little girls and lived in a relatively nice little house for Mexican standards, that is until about three months before the day I met him.

Involved in some kind of shoot out, Alexander was shot in the stomach. Before the bullet went all the way through his body, it managed to sever his spinal column. Alexander felt his legs for the very last time just before he hit the ground after being shot.

He survived the shooting and the hospital but no longer able to work, he soon found himself in hot water with the very cartel he had been employed by. When he couldn't pay his bills, he began receiving threats. Afraid her children would be held for ransom and that she would be forced to work in a brothel, Alexander's wife kicked him out of her house and filed for divorce. She moved as far away from him as possible, never to be seen again.

Now Alexander lived in a trash dump. Unable to escape the cartel, the dump, or the chair he was living in, he let his shoeless feet drag through the trash and terrible infection was all over both of his feet. He didn't care. He couldn't feel them anyway.

When it rained, the people who lived in the dump would put plastic on him and there he sat. He had lost everything a man could possibly lose. His body, his family, his home, his job, and absolutely any hope he ever had. It was bad.

On the day I met Alexander, he didn't have much to say to any of us. Mildly amused that we were there doing what we were doing, he didn't dare express any form of joy. He didn't have any to offer.So I was speaking to him while wondering how we could get him into some clean clothes and what that process might look like when I saw how badly his feet needed protecting.

"Hey man, why aren't you wearing any shoes?" I asked. He just shrugged his shoulders without saying anything. "If I get you some shoes would you wear them?" I asked. Again he just shrugged his shoulders, but this time he actually said something.

"It doesn't matter. I've got feet like an elephant and they don't have shoes my size in Mexico. I've always had to go to Texas to get my shoes and I'm not going anywhere." he said.

FEET LIKE AN ELEPHANT

Alexander didn't know it, but the term "Feet like an Elephant" was a prophetic God phrase to me. It was something I said all the time and the Holy Spirit knew it. I have always referred to my feet and two of my kids' feet as being just like an elephant because they are as wide as they are long. On the day I met this brother I was wearing a special ordered pair of size thirteen triple E shoes. So as soon as he said he had feet like an elephant, I knew my shoes would be perfect for him.

When I took off my shoes and put them on his feet, heaven invaded earth right there. This man discovered Jesus knew him and loved him the way Prince Charming discovered Cinderella. Miraculously, and precisely, the shoe fit. He knew it was Jesus.

It was a very real, very personal *miracle.*

Alexander gave his heart to Jesus that day because he was able to have hope in God's goodness.

GOOD OVERCOMES EVIL.

I preached at a very charismatic Mexican church without shoes that night. They thought it was some kind of prophetic sign so they took off their shoes too. I didn't bother to tell them anything different.

MIRACLE SHOES

The very next Friday, one week to the day I had given away my shoes in Mexico, I stood at the door of our OpenDoor Food Bank watching a fifty-two foot trailer back up from the World Vision Distribution Center. I had no idea what was in it, all I knew was that it was full of non-food items, which basically means it could be anything other than food.

It wasn't anything, it was full of one thing.

SHOES!

Over 16,000 pairs of brand new shoes were being given to me exactly *seven* days after I gave away my shoes. God is still bigger and in this case, He was showing off. I love it when God shows off. I laughed my head off and "marveled" as the Bible says, at the *goodness* of God.

THE FAT LADY SILENCED

Well, you know I thought it was over, and you know that since I'm still writing, the story isn't over. You're going to love how far this *goodness* goes.

Seven years later, I was doing a television show in Mexico. I spent an hour preaching on the goodness of God and telling really cool stories, including the one about Alexander and my elephant shoes. I was doing a three day conference in Brownsville, just across the river and I invited all the viewers and everybody who could attend, to join me for the last night, which was the next day.

My conference went the way they always go and God did amazing things. Afterwards, there were some 60-70 people lined up who wanted a personal handshake or prayer. I was tired and hungry and really wanted to get out of there quick, but I knew immediately that this was going to take a while.

At the end of the line was a guy in a suit who was watching me like NASA looks at a shuttle launch. As the line got smaller and the man got closer, I saw that his suit was not clean. In fact as he moved even closer, I could see it was filthy. As I would pray for people, I kept my eyes on him and wondered what this was going to be about. After an hour and a half of praying for people, I finally got to the very last guy in line, the guy in the dirty suit.

"I'm sorry I am so dirty," he said in Spanish. "I really wanted to look nice. I saw you on TV yesterday in Matamoros and I spent all night and all day getting across the border to be here tonight."

I instantly knew he meant that he had crossed illegally and the mud was from the river.

"No, Brother, I am so sorry it was so difficult to get to me," I said, giving him a big hug. "Why are you here to see me and what can I do for you?"

He put his hand on his mouth and told me he was very nervous. He referred to this meeting like it was a dream for him and through tears began to say, "Glory to God, glory to God! I couldn't believe it when I heard you tell the story on TV. You are the Prophet of God who put shoes on my brother's feet."

He said he had to come see me because he knew that I did not know the rest of the story.

> *"How abundant are the good things*
> *that you have stored up for those who*
> *fear you, that you bestow in the sight of all, on those*
> *who take refuge in you"*
>
> –Psalm 31:19 NIV

Alexander really had a life transforming encounter with Jesus on that hot summer day in the trash dump. Not long after, people took him into their home and he began to be about the business of getting healed from his infections and getting discipled in his new found faith in Christ.

It wasn't long after that, Alexander began having prophetic dreams. See, since I had prophetically given him my shoes and because people there called me a prophet, he just knew it was ok for him to prophesy. After all it had been part of my walk so why couldn't it be part of his walk?

He would have a dream someone was coming over. The Lord would tell him what the problem was and how to council them.

One day he dreamed his brother was coming to see him and he had a word for him.

"You are not supposed to leave your wife. You need to go back and get her and give your life to Christ. When you find her you will find out that she is now saved and is praying for you too."

The brother had no idea that Alexander knew the Lord, and he had no idea how he could have known he had left his wife months back.

When he found her, it was exactly the way Alexander had said, so they came and got him, moved him into their house, and started taking care of him.

Other dreams began to happen and other people began to show up at their house saying they had been instructed in a dream to find him. It was like Acts chapter 9, Acts chapter 10, Acts chapter 16 and Acts chapter 18 all over again.

> *In a dream, in a vision of the night, when deep sleep falls upon men, while slumbering upon their beds; [16]Then he opens the ears of men, and seals their instruction,*
>
> –Job 33:15-16

And he knew they were coming and would tell his brother.

"There is someone coming this morning who will want to give us money, but we can't spend it because the family that is coming after her will need the exact amount of money we have. The third party that is coming today will give us enough food and supplies to get us through the next several months."

And it would happen just like he told them it would happen.

"Many times," his brother said, "he would have a dream and write out all of the things God told him to tell people before they even came to the house."

"God showed me a man in a badge is coming today and when he does, hand him this letter I wrote from the Lord to him. Don't let him in to talk to me because he will make an idol out of my gift." Two hours later a federal police officer knocked on the door and the brother, by now the Pastor of the house church they had started, handed him a note.

"God told us you were coming and this note is for you." It read something like this:

"MANUEL, I AM REAL AND I LOVE YOU. TURN TO ME NOW AND LIVE WITH ME. I HAVE LIFE FOR YOU. TURN FROM IDOLS AND SALVATION IS COMING TO YOUR HOUSE TODAY.
JESUS, NO OTHER NAME."

He went on to tell me story after story of the incredible way God had used him through the years to bring miraculous transformation to so many people.

"I would love to see him, can I come to your house?" I asked, like a little kid. That's when he told me that he had just passed away not even a week earlier. He died in his bed, surrounded by people who loved him and respected him, reading his Bible and holding onto those shoes I had given him.

"He would want you to have this. I had to bring it to you," he said and he handed me a bible, Alexander's bible. It was in a large baggy to keep the water of the river he swam, out of its pages. I took it out, smelled it and held it close.

A life transformed. Hundreds of people saved. The *goodness* of God had overcome the worst evil had to throw at Alexander.

GOOD OVERCOMES EVIL

The story continues. My wife runs an amazing organization called *SPARKworldwide.org*. Just one of the incredible things she participates in is the ongoing partnership we have with that same little church. We support them on a monthly basis and part of our funding goes to a weekly food outreach to the children in that war torn region. It's something like an all day vacation bible school where the kids are fed, protected, and taught the love of Jesus through the goodness of God, demonstrated through Alexander's brother and sister-in-law.

It's affecting the whole area. See, the goodness of God, even if it's just through a pair of shoes from a guy with fat feet, overcomes the worst evil imaginable. It doesn't stop because God doesn't stop being good.

You probably know by now what I am about to say.

GOOD OVERCOMES EVIL.

"If you do good, people will accuse you of selfish ulterior motives.
Do good anyway."
–Kent M. Keith, *The Silent Revolution:*
Dynamic Leadership in the Student Council

CHAPTER 3

GOODNESS IS BIGGER

Learning to celebrate and to make a big deal out of goodness

My geographical bucket list has taken me to some amazing places. I climbed all over the great Pyramid in Egypt. Threw a coin in the Trevi Fountain in Rome. Cried out to Jesus at the Wailing Wall in Jerusalem. Put my hands on the rocks at Stonehenge. Kissed my wife in front of the Taj Mahal. I have skipped rocks across the Amazon River. I have stepped down the pilgrim's steps in Plymouth and even made my own pilgrimage to Graceland in Memphis. Hallelujah!

Listen, I am barely scratching the surface. I have seriously traveled. I have been in at least thirty-nine nations and some of them more than 100 times. I spend a third of my year, every year, stomping around the world. There is no moss on this old stone.

A big huge and major player on my magnificent bucket list was to see Mount St. Helens.

A BIG KIND OF BAD

Notorious, deadly, beautiful mesmerizing Mount St. Helens. Most notorious for its catastrophic eruption on May 18, 1980, it was the wonder of my childhood.

I was thirteen-years-old when it went off and it was a game changer for me. That was the year I really started reading, because I couldn't get enough information about what had happened.

I think this famous volcano and my hormones were erupting at about the same level, and I needed something besides the girls in my 8th grade class to get my attention. Mount St. Helens almost did it.

So here I was, thirty-four years later, standing at the Johnston Ridge Observatory, looking across at the smoking ruin of what had once been the Mount Fugi of America.

Past the smoke of the blast, there is something most people don't know about. The eruption was amazing but that's not the really big deal about Mount St. Helens. It was the landslide. It was he largest landslide in human history where a mountain moved for seventeen miles and took fifty-seven people with it.

EARTH MOVER

At 8:32 a.m., an earthquake centered directly below the north slope hit hard and about ten seconds later, the entire north part of the mountain began to move.

Traveling at 150 miles an hour and more than 1,000 feet high, it hit Spirit Lake. That's where most people think Harry R. Truman, the famous innkeeper, was fishing that morning. If he was on the lake, he was thrown at least 600 feet (60 stories) in the air, with the rest of the water, when the lake was suddenly displaced by the mountain. He had to see it coming, and then he may have gotten an ariel view before he took his last breath.

When he came down he hit something, something he is now under, somewhere.

I like Harry Truman, and knowing God is not subject to time I pray for his last moments. I pray that he's full of more peace than panic. That he knows the presence of God and somehow thinks it's awesome he has a front row seat to such an event. I pray God gave him grace for that.

Six miles further, part of the landslide hit a 1,152 foot high ridge and actually spilled over it. The mountain moved for a total of seventeen amazing miles before it finally stopped.

I looked over at the new Spirit Lake. It's about 300 feet higher than where it was the morning Harry sat calmly fishing in 1980. He saw something that only he and God know anything about. I couldn't help but wonder.

It was bad. It was really bad and I was fascinated with it.

GO GO GODZILLA

Our flesh is naturally attracted and fascinated with evil. There is something about us that wants to be really impressed with bad. It's why we love it when Tony Montana says, "Say hello to my little friend," before he blasts something through his bedroom door at the people about to murder him. I suspect it has something to do with our survival instincts and how we want to understand the things we fear.

Whatever it is, it causes the traffic in the north bound lane to slow down when there's a wreck in the south bound lane. It causes the ratings of the news media to sky rocket during disasters and the tabloid racks to go empty when a celebrity gets divorced, or when a grandfather decides to become a female sex object.

What's even more amazing, is when we can't see enough impressive bad things for us to look at, we begin to invent new forms of bad that entertain us. At first, we invent giant Krakens that take down ships and then monsters that invade whole cities. We upgrade from corporate to personal, from a monster after the city to a monster after me, and invent human feeding vampires and werewolves. Then we begin to make their horror sensual, even erotic, and we turn these monsters into romantic attractions for us. That's what we do and that's how we are. We love to love bad. It's important that we learn to no longer love as the world loves. We have to hold tight to goodness instead of evil.

> *"And do not be conformed to this world....*
> *Abhor what is evil.*
> *Cling to what is good."*
>
> –Romans 12:2, 9

A GREATER GOODNESS

God warns us and tries really hard to convince us that we have our hands on the steering wheel of our own hearts. We don't have to love bad. We can love God, and when we do we learn to love goodness because we see how incredibly good goodness really is. We can actually choose what we love and how we love if we are willing to have a higher value for one thing over the other.

God says things like, you don't want to get into "evil imaginations" (Romans 1:30). Mostly because we are good at it and we can develop huge skill sets for advancing evil and inventing new evil.

All that stuff ends up in the place designed to capture and hold evil. We don't want to be carried off into a landslide headed for hell.

But God says this, not because if we don't avoid evil it's so big and horrible it's going to get all of us. It had us before we were even born. He says this because He wants us to develop skill sets of advancing His kingdom and overcoming evil with good.

Good is much greater! Why should we be impressed with something inferior?

"Why should we be overcome with inferior evil? Why should we be defeated by a defeated devil?" as my Pastor Jim Maxwell is famous for saying. It was actually our rebellion against God that caused us to fall in love with evil and turn all of our power to it. It's why we got so hurt by evil.

> *But he who fails to find me injures himself; all who hate me love death.*
> –Proverbs 8:36 ESV

When we fall in love with God, we begin to lose our childish infatuation with evil. We learn to turn a cold shoulder to our romantic notions of darkness, and discover the true adventure of falling in love with God's *goodness.* Falling in love with Jesus is always the answer.

SEEMINGLY BIGGER BAD

We have to be careful not to make too big of a deal out of evil. I have seen darkness and evil that, for lack of a better term, was impressive. Really scary stuff that if I wasn't careful, could press something into me that is toxic to my kingdom advancement.

I have been in Idi Amins torture chamber under his palace in Kampala, Uganda. I was a murder factory where something like 100,000 people had their lives stolen from them in unspeakable horror.

Statistics indicate that at least sixty percent of Ugandans are Christians and six percent are Muslims. In spite of this, Amin declared his nation a Muslim state. Christians, both Catholics and Protestants, were at the top of the list for execution, torture, and unprecedented terror. And I'm talking about just plain demonically creative ways to terrorize people.

The two tribes, the Lambi and Acholi, predominantly Christian, bore the brunt of Amin's wrath. I have been in that place and have personally seen the blood on the walls and it's not something you just shrug your shoulders at. You taste it and it's hard not to feel tiny against such huge evil. That torture chamber is full of dark filth and hopeless ruin.

I know first hand what has happened to my friends in Mexico who survived being kidnapped by the cartel. I know what happened to their kids. Things I will not write about.

I have stood on a mass grave of 250,000 people who were hacked to death in Rwanda.

I have stood on the banks of a river in Uganda where Anglican pastors were tied up and fed to crocodiles because they loved Jesus.

I have been to the torture chambers of Pablo Escobar in Columbia and stood where he had federal judges murdered.

I was in a brothel in India and walked past padlocked doors where I knew girls were being held against their will. I bought a twelve-year-old for $60 who was so traumatized she was emotionally dead.

Yeah, I know what I'm talking about when I say it's easy to give into the compulsion to have a reverence or some kind of great feeling of horrible wonder at such huge evil.

That is a big mistake. It's a lie. It's just how our heads work. While it is a big deal what happens to people, the evil that does it is really no big deal at all. I don't deny the evil you have been reading about, I deny the powerful influence of such a thing.

THE HOBBIT OF EVIL

There is really nothing impressive about evil. Amin is just one of the most recent headliners in a long line of tyrants who've played their demonic roles in history. The brutality of Idi Amin is solid evidence that man's basic condition is still the same as it has always been. Man's heart is still deceitful and wicked, and still desperately in need of a Savior. There is nothing impressive about that at all. Idi Amin was a pathetic muslim punk with daddy issues. Same old song and dance.

From a kingdom perspective, evil is something to be judged and to be executed with extreme prejudice. We are not to be impressed with it, we are to overcome it with good.

What should blow us all away is that the church is thriving in Uganda and people are being educated, fed, and blessed in incredible ways because of it. Uganda has been a hub to the rest of the African nations as a place of light and stability for decades now. Like the forest that began to rise up out of the ashes right after Mount St. Helens blew up, it's impressive how quickly goodness reigns over destruction.

Good overcomes evil.

Rwandan Churches have somehow mixed both tribes in the same congregations and people are loving each other as family. That's goodness overcoming hatred in a way I don't even have a dashboard for.

What is impressive is the goodness of God in the life of that little girl I redeemed and set free. We should be impressed, blown away, and stirred up by *goodness*. Fear shuts us down but goodness causes us to do something more!

THE PATHETIC PAPER TIGER OF EVIL

My good friend, singer and song writer Pauline Wick, wrote an amazing song called *Paper Tiger*. On the word that her father would certainly die from a fatal heart attack, the Lord gave her another word that said, it's not that big of a deal. The *goodness* of God overcame the evil of the heart attack.

It turns out that evil isn't all that scary after all. When cloaked in darkness, and left up to our imagination, the devil is as a roaring lion stalking the ancient campfires of traveling middle eastern people. He's the boogeyman and there is no limit as to how you can imagine him once you hear his terrible sound in the dark. When we buy into that, we give him permission to devour us. That's what Peter was talking about.

> *Be sober, be vigilant;*
> *because your adversary the devil*
> *walks about like a roaring lion,*
> *seeking whom he may devour.*
>
> –I Peter 5:8

Even Veggietales knows that "God is bigger than the boogeyman."

History proves it.

TOOTHLESS EVIL

Al Capone, the meanest, gangster bully ever, spent several years in cell 181 on Alcatraz Island. He wept so much through the nights the other inmates called him names and made fun of him. He died from the insanity and pain that syphilis and gonorrhea had brought him. His tombstone reads, "My Jesus Mercy".

The evil he had partnered with wasn't so powerful after all.

VENOM-LESS EVIL

Bonny and Clyde, John Dillenger, even Pablo Escobar were all feared as being unstoppable evil. They were also all rounded up and shot by Texans who were not afraid to chase them throughout the earth! They died thousands of miles apart, years apart, alone on a street somewhere and afterwards, people poked at their bodies.

There is nothing bullet proof about evil.

DEFENSELESS EVIL

Osama bin Laden tried to hide behind one of his wives. It didn't work. Saddam Hussein was found in a spider hole full of fleas. His palaces and fortresses blown to pieces.

Evil can not hide from Goodness.

In Kampala, Uganda, President Yoweri Museveni's spokesman called Idi Amin's death good, and he was right.

GOOD OVERCOMES EVIL

When the devil is pulled out of his spider hole and revealed to humanity in judgement, Isaiah the prophet says this in chapter 14:

> *"Those who see you will gaze at you,*
> *And consider you, saying:*
> *'Is this the man who made the earth tremble,*
> *Who shook kingdoms,*
> [17]*Who made the world as a wilderness*
> *And destroyed its cities,*
> *Who did not open the house of his prisoners?'"*
>
> –Isaiah 14 ***:16-17***

There is a gasp in the crowd, expecting a giant dragon to be pulled from the pit. Instead, a pathetic, balding nerd comes climbing out begging for his pathetic life.

What? Are you kidding me? Really?! That's the personification of all things evil? That weakling?

If the devil is obviously impotent, then where did his power come from? His power came from us. His evil had power because we cooperated with it. We held it in reverence. We even loved it at times. We propelled it and advanced it.

The devil isn't powerful because evil is powerful. The devil is powerful because we are powerful and we tend to work for him. You and I are done with that.

GOOD OVERCOMES THE HOBBIT OF EVIL.

"Do your little bit of good where you are; it's those little bits of good put together that overwhelm the world."

–Desmond Tutu

CHAPTER 4

HELPING THE HURTING

God's goodness in the lives of unwanted kids

My daughter Maegan is an extraordinary girl. She's all grown up now, married, and producing beautiful grandbabies for me. But there has always been something very, very special about Maegan.

One of the great proofs in the pudding of her specialness has to do with a mission trip when she journeyed alone to eastern India. She had been with her globe trekking daddy on several trips but this time she went by herself.

Maegan loves India like I love India. India is extreme. India is different. India is, well, uniquely India.

It's an amazing time to bring the gospel of Jesus to India. It's a window we must take advantage of. India's massive population and rapid economic growth is one of the biggest stories of the century so far, but I tell you that under all of those headlines is the reality of a very real revival beginning to happen in that amazing place.

So Maegan had a very busy schedule to keep when it was all interrupted by a tiny little orphan girl.

GIRL INTERRUPTED

At one of a blur of events there was one little girl among thousands Maegan would see that caught her attention. An orphaned little girl, dying of aids, and crying because her arm was broken. I'm not sure of the exact circumstances of how my little girl came across that little girl, but it was a game changer for Maegan.

"Daddy, nobody in the world loved her. Nobody." She told me.

To actually come across somebody that no living human being on earth loved. Nobody would help her or hear her cry of starvation and pain. Maegan did and it ruined her schedule because her compassion caused her to get personally involved in a very real and tangible way. That's what compassion does.

This is the *goodness* of God and goodness overcomes evil.

So it was with all this in mind I sat looking out of the window, 36,000 feet above the Sahara Desert. Just weeks after my daughter's trip to India, I was going to our orphanage in Uganda, East Africa.

A VOICE IN THE DESERT

The Sahara is impressive with its 3.6 million square miles of shifting sand dunes and red rocked mountains. It's north Africa's great wonder, and from that high in the air the heat makes it impossible to determine where the land ends and the sky begins. The horizon is a blur of color and it's a great show when you've got nothing to do on a very long flight.

A random memory of the little girl in India launched me into a God thought. Suddenly, I had three thoughts in a row that I recognized came from the Spirit, something like Holy Ghost flash cards. It went like this:

BOOM! Little boy, orphaned, unloved, dejected.
BOOM! Under a tree, crying, sad, helpless.
BOOM! Broken arm, pain, ongoing, anxiety.

And Just like that, I knew God had spoken to me. Somehow, somewhere, I was going to come across a little boy with a broken arm, just like my daughter, and he was going to be an orphan. I was going to help him and love him. I had a mission on my missions trip.

I turned to Leanna and told her, "God just told me something."

"What did he say?"

"We need to look for a kid with a broken arm standing under a tree," I said. "We are going to help him."

RAID ON ENTEBBE

Through the years my wife and I have been to Uganda somewhere around thirty-five times all together. I have stomped around east Africa about a dozen times and my wife more than twenty. With two children's homes in that great nation, my memory of Uganda over the past twenty years is a colorful Cajun gumbo of faces, smiles, orphans, laughter, funerals, kings, animals, traveling, preaching, and building with things like strange food and locust swarms mixed in. Incredible sickness, heartbreaking circumstances, and joyous wonder that can't even be communicated. Uganda, to me, is Africa. I love Uganda.

Now there is no way to actually describe the reality of what it's like when we arrive at our children's homes. It's a celebration that I imagine is something like your first day in heaven. You walk through a long tunnel of people on either side of you that are cheering and trying to touch you. The music is loud, the drum beats are fast, and dancing in front of you are young women and little girls in tribal dress. There are smiles and tears and hugs and laughing and it's a grand explosion of intentional celebration and reunion. Everyone is singing and everyone, sometimes nearly a thousand people, want to shake your hand and welcome you. I never get tired of it.

It was in this chaotic atmosphere of kingdom disarray that I saw him. Not even five minutes after I stepped off the bus, I looked over the heads of all my little munchkins at our children's home and spotted a little boy about twenty yards away. There he was. He was naked, he was crying, he was standing under a big African tree, and he was holding his arm. I shouted at Leanna who was only five feet away from me, but from the noise of the party we were walking through, she couldn't understand what I was saying.

"There he is!" I shouted. "The kid from the plane!"

"The kid from the what?" she questioned.

"The kid God told me about on the plane. Look, there he is!"

When Leanna turned to see the kid I was pointing at, everything changed. A moment later and she had abandoned the welcome celebration and was holding a kid who was terrified of the first white person he had ever seen. I could see by the gestures she was making and the huge frown on her face that the little boy did have a broken arm. It was just like God had said:

BOOM! Little boy, orphaned, unloved, dejected.
BOOM! Under a tree, crying, sad, helpless.
BOOM! Broken arm, pain, ongoing, anxiety.

And Just like that, I knew God had derailed us into this little boy's life. Leanna was going to help him and love him. Our missions trip had a whole new mission. I had a mission.

God sees the evil that is done to the orphaned. Good overcomes evil.

NEVER ENDING AND EVER GOING

My wife and I, through Leanna's ministry, *SPARKworldwide.org* will continue to help thousands of little boys and girls literally all over the world. This is not just a plug for that ministry, it's a plug for the heart of Jesus towards people that people do not care about.

When we get to heaven there will be no meaning or place to words like abandoned or fatherless or rejected or shamed. A really good way to see heaven invade earth right now is to make your business to see those same people received, fathered, accepted, and honored. Now. Right now. Right this very moment without anymore delay.

GOOD OVERCOMES EVIL.

"The very fact that a holy, eternal, all-knowing, all-powerful, merciful, fair, and just God loves you and me is nothing short of astonishing."

–Francis Chan

CHAPTER 5

THE WORK OF GOODNESS

Goodness is something that must be done

There is a beautiful scene near the end of *The Agony and the Ecstasy,* Irving Stone's historical novel about Michelangelo. An ailing Pope Julius II visits the nearly completed ceiling of the Sistine Chapel. Michelangelo has to help him up the last few rungs of the ladder. He looks above him at Michelangelo's depiction of God, about to impart the gift of life to Adam.

This Pope had fought terrible, bloody wars in the name of the church. He has blood on his hands, and he isn't even sure if his cause had been successful. But as he looks at Michelangelo's picture of God, a smile comes to his cracked lips.

"Do you truly believe God is that benign?" The Pope asks the artist.

Michelangelo replies, "Yes, Holy Father."

Pope Julius says, "I most ardently hope so, since I am going to be standing before Him before long. If He is as you have painted Him, then I shall be forgiven my sins."

In Michelangelo's painting, the Pope saw a different image of God, unlike the one he had lived with his whole life. It never occurred to him that God loved to give life. This God, that he was getting a revelation of, wasn't killing life, He was giving life. This God was a giver even in the face of his sins.

That famous painting, you know, the one where the strong finger of God is reaching out to touch the limp-wristed hand of Adam, actually started a revival that would ruin the Catholic's cornered market on the church. When people saw that image, painted high, as if you were looking into heaven, a new revelation of the *goodness* of God actually giving life, began to burst into the hearts of people. Something that would later turn into the major parts of the reformation.

THE END OF THE LINE

I was stomping around in Rome. My wife and I were going to do a two week Mediterranean cruise with two good friends and I saw this long line of people. Tourists were there from every corner of the very round globe. Fat ones and skinny ones. Typical Americans with loud colored shirts and big hats, suave Europeans with small sunglasses and tight dark clothes, Japanese tourists with tons of cameras and selfie sticks. All of them tourists.

"What the heck is that?" I asked out loud after the third or fourth city block of this long line of people.

"This is the line to see the Sistine Chapel." The taxi driver said, just minutes before he would try hard to rip me off. I think it's part of the code of conduct for Italians who work the tourists near the Colosseum.

But according to TripAdvisor, waiting in line without a guided tour can take an entire day before you are herded through for a break neck glance. And what is everybody trying so hard to see? A master's piece of art? Yes, but also a Renaissance depiction of a vision of God's *goodness* as a life giving Father. Michelangelo nailed it in more ways than one. The goodness of God gives life.

A fundamental truth of the *goodness* of God is that Goodness is life giving.

BUTTERFLY KISSES

My kids are not the most artistic bunch, but when they were little they would do like most kids and often make a crayon masterpiece. Sometimes they would be thrilled to bring me what some would consider less than flattering circles with heads on them. I would pretend it was not because they saw me as fat but because they were at some early stage of development.

I'm no psychologist but I would observe the houses were always whole and so were the hearts. That was a big deal to me because so many little people in our children's church draw pictures that would make us bawl. Kids we know with broken homes would draw half houses where the other runs off the page and you can't see it. I guessed they couldn't see the other half of their real house. Or they would draw a picture of the new family and leave themselves out of the group or really sad suns or things like that.

All my kids were loved and a little on the spoiled side of a family that has a really big emphasis on family. So when my youngest daughter, for example, would bring me a picture she would often say, "Look Daddy, it's you!" She couldn't get it into my hands quick enough. She would wait for my reaction and I would do something silly like put my hand on my chest and yell out, "Good googly moogly! I want to paint that vision on the great wall of China!"

She would laugh and run off to draw something else because she couldn't wait to get another crazy response out of me. I miss those days.

THE PORTRAITS WE PAINT

As a Christian I think I still do that kind of thing to my spiritual father. I give to Him little moments and eventually a life I think looks like Him. The life we live is an open demonstration of what we believe about God. You do that unto the Lord and it's just like giving Him something that says, "It's you, Daddy!"

If you have a revelation about what an awesome giver the Lord is, you will find yourself being a giver in your church or helping someone in a bad financial place. That's you running to the Father, handing Him your service, and saying, "This looks like you, Daddy."

No fear of criticism. No fear of taking it to Him. He's a good dad and every time you get an incredible response from the Father, you feel like the most loved person on the planet.

So people line up to look at the painting they have heard so much about and I tell you the portrait that most of us have painted looks more like the scream than the ceiling in the chapel.

UNFINISHED WORKS

Did you know that da Vinci never finished the Mona Lisa? Did you know there are two of them? Do a Google search on the second Mona Lisa and you'll see what I'm talking about.

Our portrait of Jesus might look more like the Mona Lisa than anything else because we are not really sure if God actually smiles or not. It is absolutely evident to me, and anybody with a third grade education, the church at large has not been totally convinced of God's goodness and because of that we have not been known for being life giving.

We have a lot of work in the church to finish the painting of God's goodness. Yes, it's ok to put a smile on the face of Jesus because He really is good!

GOD SMILES WHEN HE GIVES

The giving side of God shows up as goodness and looks like increase.

> *Yes, the Lord will give what is good; And our land will yield its increase.*
>
> –Psalm 85:12

When God gives to us, His intention is to fill us up with goodness. He has a huge agenda to see goodness in your life.

> *What You give them they gather in; You open Your hand, they are filled with good.*
>
> –Psalm 104:28

Our tiny ability to imitate God in giving goodness to those we love is not even on the same scale as God's giving nature of goodness.

> *If you then, being evil, know how to give good gifts to your children, how much more will your Father who is in heaven give good things to those who ask Him!*
>
> –Matthew 7:11

When God gives to you, even the measure is called good.

> *"Give, and it will be given to you: good measure, pressed down, shaken together, and running over will be put into your bosom. For with the same measure that you use, it will be measured back to you."*
>
> –Luke 6:38

God takes pleasure and actually enjoys giving to you, and when He does it's called good pleasure.

> *"Do not fear, little flock, for it is your Father's good pleasure to give you the kingdom."*
>
> –Luke 12:32

God's *goodness* always gives away life.

> *"I am the good shepherd. The good shepherd gives His life for the sheep."*
>
> –John 10:11

This is because goodness, like the love of God, is always selfless.

So the thing you need to know about goodness is that when it shows up it is always life giving. And the thing is, it should show up everywhere Christ is present or the bride of Christ is activated. The overcoming, devil stomping, hopelessness destroying, life giving, fruit bearing *goodness* of God.

It's why we at OpenDoor feed 50,000 people a year here in Johnson County through our food bank. It's why we treat them like kings in the way we feed them. We want people to know that God is good. It's why we here at *SPARKworldwide.org* take care of so many children here and throughout the world. People, hear me on this, God is *good*. It really is that simple and that simple message changes everything. Especially when that message is not just preached but actually demonstrated.

As I said before, God's *goodness* is seen in one less victim of abuse, one less addict, one less dropout, and one less suicide. God's *goodness* is seen in one more restoration, one more transformation, and one more person walking into something better and higher for their life.

GOODNESS IS SOMETHING YOU DO

Goodness is both the motivation and the result of doing something.

> *They are to do good, to be rich in good works, to be generous and ready to share.*
>
> –I Timothy 6:18 ESV

> *So then, as we have opportunity, let us do good to everyone, and especially to those who are of the household of faith.*
>
> –Galatians 6:10 ESV

YOU DO GOODNESS WHEN GOD IS WITH YOU

When God is with us we do good. We don't just talk good or look good or act good we DO good.

> *How God anointed Jesus of Nazareth with the Holy Ghost and with power: who went about doing good, and healing all that were oppressed of the devil; for God was with him.*
>
> –Acts 10:38 KJV

When we live in a constant awareness of God's presence we DO good. From God's presence we do more than preach good but actually DO good because of our supernatural confidence and courage. That goodness we do overcomes evil and undoes darkness.

POSERS VS. ACTORS

The early church was not a community of people who sat on their blessed assurance and wished or hoped in a very good God. They believed and they acted upon it. Their actions changed everything, and according to Acts 17:6 they had a reputation of overturning everything in the world. Motivated by the *goodness* of God, they took on hell with a Holy Ghost water pistol and shook the foundations of Rome itself!

The fifth book of the New Testament records the courageous and miraculous deeds of our forefathers, and do you know what? It's not called, *The Theology of the Apostles.* It's not titled, *The Opinions or the Prayers of the Apostles.* It's called THE ACTS OF THE APOSTLES.

Goodness is what they actually did. In living out and carrying out goodness, they brought the gospel of the kingdom and the presence of Jesus into the lives of untold numbers of human beings now for 2,000 years.

Goodness, as an action, can be best described as destroying the works of the devil.

> *"He that committeth sin is of the devil; for the devil sinneth from the beginning. For this purpose the Son of God was manifested, that he might destroy the works of the devil."*
>
> –I John 3:8 KJV

If *goodness* is what we do then darkness goes away and the brightness of God can not be quenched.

GOOD OVERCOMES EVIL.

"Lord of hosts! When I swim in the merciful waters of your grace I find that I can neither plumb nor measure the depths."

–Menno Simons

CHAPTER 6

FEEDING THE HUNGRY

Miracles happen in the context of serving

One of the most obvious and blatant examples of God's *goodness* around those of us who live life together, continues to be the stories that come from the OpenDoor Food Bank.

Let me tell you some of my most favorite manifestations of God's amazing heart that I have seen first hand with my own two eyes. When I say that good overcomes evil and we need to make a place and make a big deal out of God's *goodness*, I say it because I know for a fact what happens when we do. God is God on this earth as He is in heaven. Even if it's just for a tiny glimpse, like in the day of Moses when He showed him His glory, His *goodness* passing before us is a game changer.

GAME CHANGER

I was young. Still young enough to feel the need to impress my father-in-law. So when Ray Knight called me and told me what to do, I did it.

"There's an old man roofing his own roof. You ought to go help him," he said. "I'll be about directly and come help you."

Here's the skinny on a very fat story.

The old man was eighty-four-years-old. A World War II veteran, he lived in a community of mostly isolated, elderly people in the far western part of Ft Worth, Texas. The roof he was working on had leaked for years, and determined to fix it he would daily hammer down one solitary shingle. He couldn't carry a bundle. He could barely climb the ladder, and by the time he got up there the sun would be high in the sky and he would need to rest.

After nailing down one shingle he would sit for a long time watching cars drive by and contemplating his death defying trip back down the ladder. It took him twice as long to get down than it did to climb up, so by the time it was over, so was the day.

He had spent an entire season on a small patch of roof and would likely spend his last remaining years accomplishing this vision, until the *goodness* of God showed up.

JACOB'S LADDER

I slung a bundle on my shoulder and climbed the ladder. I said some kind of good morning but he didn't say anything back. I think he thought I worked for the city and was going to inspect him somehow.

I hammered down the first sixteen shingles and four bundles later, I had finished my first square. Within a few hours Ray and several of his friends and family were all hammering nails and moving up and down the ladder like Jacob's busy dream. It didn't take long before the top of the house was all brand new.

"Well sir, your roof is all done. How about them apples?" I said in my typical hick accent.

"It ain't my roof," he replied, in an accent way worse than mine. "It's my girlfriend's."

We all started laughing and not long after, we were helping him down the ladder to meet the owner of the house.

When she opened the door, I was staggered by how old this sweet lady was. Older than a century and apparently with lots of mileage, she reminded me of the Ancient of Days.

She hugged me, invited us inside, and offered us lemonade. When she opened her refrigerator door, my wife Leanna saw that it was almost completely empty. Besides a few condiments there was not food to speak of that would make a meal. Leanna whispered to me, "I'm going to go to the grocery store and bring back some food."

I was in my mid twenties back then, plus I had already been at this house for about five hours. "Please don't leave me here with these old people. I'll go to the store and you stay here."

"Nope." And with that Leanna was out the door.

About an hour later, after hearing the same story at least fifteen times, the love of my life arrived with three big bags of groceries.

The sweet old lady was so grateful she began crying. "This is the greatest day of my life," she kept saying. "A new roof and lots of food. Thank You Jesus, thank You Jesus!"

With as much excitement as she could muster, she expressed her joy over such a surprise. In kind, with as much contempt as the grumpy old man could muster, he expressed his indignation. Not only was he not getting any credit for the roof being done, he was not getting any groceries.

"Well, what about me?" The old man blurted. "I ain't got no food either."

The room got quiet and we listened to more of his complaints for a little while.

"Well, since you're so sweet," I said getting up, "let's take you down to Kroger."

Of course the old codger wasn't through. "Well, I've got another girl friend across the street who is way poorer than this old woman. We need to get her some groceries, too."

Ten minutes later, we were across the street, standing on another lady's porch and offering to take her to the grocery store.

She was embarrassed but grateful. "I have a sweet friend behind me who really needs help. Can we take her as well?"

THE PLAYER

I could see real quick where this was going. I decided to offer to come back on the weekend with enough food for everybody. I told them to gather their elderly friends together and meet me in that same front yard at 10:00 on Saturday morning.

The old man had a lot of girl friends and all of them were just barely surviving.

I worked on it all week and on Saturday morning my bride and I loaded up all of my kids, including my infant twins, and headed to town with enough food for at least a dozen people.

When we arrived I couldn't believe what was standing in front of me. More than thirty-five people stood out front of a little worn down house, drinking coffee, and speaking together like they were waiting for a bus to the casino.

When I pulled into the driveway, they started lining up and right there, I knew that *Jehovah Sneaky* had just given me a powerful ministry. I didn't know how big it was going to be but I certainly had a Holy Spirit "Uh Oh" moment.

I found out that day there were many in the same neighborhood who were not healthy enough to leave the house. In a matter of weeks, Leanna and the kids and I were taking groceries and personally visiting seventy-one isolated, elderly people every single Saturday.

We did that for over 2 years before officially starting OpenDoor Fellowship Ministries, which would later include OpenDoor Church, and eventually the OpenDoor Food Bank that gives away millions of pounds of food to tens of thousands every year now.

MIRACLE MAKER

It turns out that all that goodness is the catalyst for incredible miracles and transformation. Goodness always has selflessness attached to it. Selflessness always has the love of God attached to it, and with the love of God comes grace to overcome everything.

> *LOVE...*
> *bears all things, believes all things,*
> *hopes all things, endures all things.*
> *Love never fails. . . .*
>
> –I Corinthians 13:7-8 (emphasis mine) NASB

Did you know that with the power to serve, comes the supernatural power to overcome things? See, the *goodness* of God that overcomes evil starts off as a willingness to serve but ends up as a transformational juggernaut.

Heaven's momentum comes from faithfully serving and so does heaven's authority!

> *But you are not to be like that.*
> *Instead, the greatest among you*
> *should be like the youngest,*
> *and the one who rules like the one who serves*
>
> –Luke 22:26 NIV

In the kingdom, authority is servant authority. When people are selflessly serving others the Crown of Heaven and the Prince of Peace both show up.

WOWS AND WONDERS

In well over twenty years of consistently bringing God's goodness to the poor and afflicted, we have seen miracles beyond definition. Some of the greatest miracles I have ever seen have just naturally happened while we were helping people very practically.

Acts 2:22 is the only verse in the whole Bible that mentions all three ways heaven openly invades earth: signs, miracles, and wonders. This should get your attention if God has been waking you up at 2:22 or if you have been seeing 222 everywhere.

I am going to give you my simple version of the difference between these three levels of the Holy Spirit being made manifest.

SIGNS : A sign is a natural event that works like a supernatural billboard. It proclaims a message and symbolically points to something else unseen. A sign is when God uses the natural to proclaim the supernatural. It doesn't take much of a skill set to see a sign, but just because you know God is speaking doesn't mean that you know what He is saying. Nor does it mean that you know what to do with such a word. These are more mature and developed skill sets that come from the heart of true seekers. When it comes to signs only people that are looking even see them.

MIRACLES : Whereas a sign is when God uses the natural, a miracle is when God changes the natural with the supernatural. When God intervenes and changes the natural from what they are to what they should be, we call those things miracles. People can argue for other explanations because that is their agenda but God's people know better.

WONDERS : A wonder is a jaw dropper. It's when even righteous people don't have words or explanation. It's when God does something that might take you decades to find a scripture for it. A wonder makes you rethink everything. A wonder is always attached to how wonderful God is, and raises the bar for new levels of faith and experience with Him. When we see wonders among us, we find a whole new grid for walking with God that we didn't even know existed. We step out from the confines of our limited theology and walk right off the map of things that made sense to us before.
Depending upon your maturity and how well versed you are at having God completely rock your world, your personal wonder may be that you heard God speak or it may be you were found in another place and have no explanation as to how you got there. It may be that you were healed or maybe that you were invited to spend time with a British Lord on a Virgin Island to have godly influence in an ungodly environment. It may be you happen to find the long lost relative of somebody you have prayed for or it may be that somebody gives you a five million dollar building without ever asking for it.

I have had all of those wonders personally happen to me at different times in my life and all of them changed the grid for me. A wonder will make you sit there and stare at the wall or in Ezekiel's case, the river.

Then I came to them of the captivity at Telabib,
that dwelt by the river of Chebar,
and I sat where they sat,
and remained there astonished
among them seven days.

–Ezekiel 3:15 KJV

If you haven't had a mind blowing wonder and game changing encounter with the Lord Jesus Christ, well Neighbor, as the Wolf Brand Chili commercial used to say, "That's too long."

You need a *goodness* of God injection to bring the wonders of the Lord back into your life again. Let me give you my top ten list of favorite wonders that have happened while seeing the *goodness* of God among the poorest people around me.

HEALED OF BLINDNESS

A little boy named Joshua who was born blind was healed of blindness while we were feeding a tiny remote village in India. We had at least a dozen witnesses from OpenDoor that saw this miracle happen. Good overcomes the evil of darkness.

JUST IN THE NICK OF TIME

The IRS voluntarily sent me $1700 back in 1996 after an internal audit. The $1700 was exactly the amount of money I needed to keep me from loosing my little house and it came in on the very last day I had to send the money to the mortgage company. I had no idea it was coming but good overcomes evil that comes against our homes.

AIDS HAS GOTTA GO

In 1998, a good friend of mine named Mike Duffy was in the last stages of full blown AIDS. At a special healing service where we invited all of our outreach recipients, it was there that Mike Duffy told me God had just healed him. He began to improve immediately and when he went to the doctor they could find no trace of AIDS in his body. He eventually got so healthy he rode his bicycle over 300 miles in one single riding. Good overcomes the evil of terrible diseases.

I HAVE NEVER EVEN HEARD OF ANYTHING LIKE THIS

On a missions trip to Uganda, East Africa in 2010 with a medical team, we came across a little girl with Down syndrome at one of our clinics. A registered American nurse spent time with the mama trying to explain the challenges she would have in the future with raising her child in the village. We fed them, clothed them, and prayed for them. The next year we came back with the very same nurse and we found the very same family at another village gathering. To our wonder, God had completely healed that little girl and she had no symptoms, signs, or difficulties of Down syndrome anymore. Even her physical features had changed.

Good overcomes the evil of birth defects.

LOAVES AND FISHES

On a missions trip to Brownsville, Texas in 2006, we took 1,000 backpacks stuffed full of brand new toys to the Mexican border for a Christmas children's outreach. Successfully advertised, our event brought in more than 3,000 little boys and girls. We fed everybody and preached the gospel as we face painted and handed out backpacks. About an hour and a half into the event, our entire team began to become aware of a tremendous miracle. After giving away thousands of backpacks our truck was still full! Even after handing out more than 3,000 backpacks to over 3,000 registered children, our truck was still completely full at the end of the night. We sent them across the border to other partner churches. We only took 1,000 down there and we have no idea where the rest of them came from. Good overcomes the evil of child poverty.

A BEAUTIFUL FACE

After seeing a woman who received food from us for over a year, I asked her why she always hid her face from me. She was a beautiful lady and I suspected that someone might have been beating her up because she looked at the ground and kept her hair in front of her face. She pulled back her hair and showed me a terrible cancerous place on her left cheek. Because she was an illegal immigrant, she was too afraid to go to the hospital and she immediately began to cry about it saying it's getting worse and worse. I reached over and put my hand on her face saying a simple prayer and asking God to heal her. When the palm of my hand touched her face she reacted and turned her head quickly. The growth got hung in a ring I was wearing and when she jerked, it yanked right off and fell into my hand. Her cancer literally fell off into my hand! Her cheek looked perfect and all of the food bank volunteers came to step on the cancer in the parking lot. Good overcomes the evil of cancer.

A MULTIMILLION DOLLAR CAMPUS

On June 12, 2011, I stood before an arbitrator and a church board that was trying to shut down every outreach ministry I had, including the food bank and our orphanages. Convinced that I was reckless and irresponsible by a woman who wanted to control and limit all things at OpenDoor, the board told the arbitrator I had brought in that if it was up to me, I would give away every dime the church had to people who would never even go to our church. Even though she was an employee of mine, she would not allow it. She actually said that my giving to the poor could be considered stealing because it was so detrimental to the church bank account. My church elders confronted the Jezebel spirit and hateful slander of the whole group and all of them left us, doing as much damage as they could possibly do on their way out. I barely survived the attack but by the grace of God we bounced back and started helping people more than ever.

Two years later to the exact day of that terrible meeting, on June 12, 2013, a pastor in a neighboring city asked me to visit her in her office. Announcing she wanted to retire she said she wanted to give me something. Even though we were not affiliated in any way or had ever done ministry together, she said God told her to find me, have her church merge with mine, and to give me all of the property she had that included, what I think, is the nicest church building in the city and a sanctuary that potentially holds 1,400 people. A campus worth millions of dollars was given to me on the exact day I had been accused of terrible things because I help the poor. Good overcomes the evil of religion and slander.

NEW FLOOR, NEW WALLS, AND NEW ROOF

In 1993 I prayed with a sweet old lady I took groceries to every Saturday. She always met me out on the porch and was not comfortable with me even getting close to the front door. Concerned she was afraid of me, I asked her about it and she told me that the inside of her house was ruined and she was embarrassed. After decades of a leaky roof, her walls were molded and her wood floors were badly warped. I prayed with her and put together a team that would fix her house but I never had to because God did a wonder!

The very next Saturday when I returned she had a new roof, new walls, and a new floor throughout her house. On the Monday after we prayed, the city was putting up a new transformer next to her house and the electrical pole fell and crashed into her living room. When the Mayor of the small town saw the condition of her house he put together a team of more than 100 people and construction crews to completely redo everything. Good overcomes the evil of a widow's poverty!

PERFECT TIMING AND A GREAT BALL GAME

Sometime around 1990 I was preaching in a prison in far east Texas. I met a guy who told me he had been saved for about a year but had no way to communicate it to his family. He said that his brother had sent him a bible and wrote in it that he should read the red letters and several years later he actually did and gave his life to Christ. The problem was that he had lost all communication with his family and there was no way for him to find his brother. I prayed that God would do a miracle and wrote down his name in my prayer journal.

The next day I was 200 miles away from there, at The Ball Park in Arlington, watching a Texas Rangers game. After a brief and polite conversation with the stranger sitting next to me, I mentioned I had been in a particular prison unit the night before. He told me he had a brother in that same unit. The incredible miracle is that this guy sitting next to me was the very same person I had prayed for to be reconnected to his brother, just the night before. Wow! Goodness overcomes the evil of estrangement and alienation.

THE HANNAH MONTANA MIRACLE

In the first few years of our church, a beautiful little girl named Angel touched the heart of my wife. Her family was really struggling and we were reaching out to them in every way we could. It was Christmas time and we knew we wanted to bless her and her siblings with a very special Christmas so we asked her to pray with us about it. In the cutest little voice I ever heard she said, "Jesus, please give me a nice Hannah Montana dress and God bless Hannah Montana."

Obviously, we were going to get that kid some Hannah Montana stuff but I didn't have to, because goodness passed before us. About 3 days later our local Wal-Mart Distribution Center donated a truck of toys and you already know what kind they were. Hanna Montana hats, underwear, socks, dresses, pants, shirts, sunglasses, lunch boxes, and on and on. A fifty-two foot semi trailer with all things Hanna Montana showed up at the supernatural request of a little girl. Before I gave any of it away, I let her pick out anything she wanted and as much as she wanted because good overcomes the evil of child poverty.

So when I say that spiritual authority shows up in the context of serving, I know what I am talking about. Goodness is such a big deal that God's response is lavish and over the top. I love it when God shows off when He shows us His glory. Remember, it's in that context He causes his *goodness* to pass before us.

> *So the Lord said to Moses, "I will also do this thing that you have spoken; for you have found grace in My sight, and I know you by name."*
>
> *And he said, "Please, show me Your glory."*
>
> *Then He said, "I will make all My goodness pass before you, and I will proclaim the name of the Lord before you. I will be gracious to whom I will be gracious, and I will have compassion on whom I will have compassion."*
>
> –Exodus 33:17-20

GOOD OVERCOMES EVIL.

"Is he – quite safe? I shall feel rather nervous about meeting a lion." "Safe?" said Mr. Beaver. "Who said anything about safe? 'Course he isn't safe! But he's good. He's the king, I tell you."

–C.S. Lewis, *The Chronicles of Narnia*

CHAPTER 7

THE EXPERIENCE OF GOODNESS

The atmosphere, environments, and outcomes of goodness

Ok, now this chapter is going to be way, way out there. I'm an atmosphere fanatic. I haven't always been like that. When I was a kid everything I did looked like someone was moving hell and I was the very first load. My physical appearance was a mess. My room looked like a 747 had failed at a crash landing. My school locker was filled from the bottom to the very top with magazines, guitar pieces, old clothes, and unspeakable things that would grow and multiply in the dark. There was very little order in my messed up world, and my world was messed up because of it.

Something happened when I got saved. I began to appreciate the value of stewarding environments and creating atmospheres. With a world famous version of ADHD, although I am too old to have the H anymore, I have learned to be very intentional about the kind of surroundings I keep myself in. I learned this from Jesus.

God created a beautiful and life giving environment for Adam in the Garden. He produced a fiery and thunderous environment to bring the law to the mountain for Moses. He fashioned stillness to bring His intimate voice to Elijah. See, the context of setting is very important to produce a specific outcome. God knows this and so does the Devil. Paul refers to this in the book of Ephesians.

> *Wherein in time past ye walked according*
> *to the course of this world,*
> *according to the prince of the power of the air,*
> *the spirit that now worketh in the children of disobedience:*
>
> –Ephesians 2:2 KJV

The spirit that is working in ungodly people is all about control for the air or the atmosphere. People don't know that so they unknowingly turn over a big part of their lives to the enemy because of it. How many churches have taught the Bible but were horrible stewards of their atmosphere? How many daddies made sure their kids went to church, but when he came home the atmosphere of the house was such that everybody had to walk on pins and needles?

Fear, anxiety, depression, heartache, regret, outrage, offense, anything carnally charged, or sexed up is the kind of nest that hell drops it's sinister eggs into. The prince from hell wants that to be the atmosphere of your head, your heart, your body, and your home. That's why when Jesus shows up as a prince, He's called the *Prince of Peace* (Isaiah 9:6). Jesus is always the answer. So it's important to steward atmospheres and set tones.

GOODNESS ULTIMATELY CHANGES THE ENVIRONMENT AND ATMOSPHERE.

When you get good at setting atmosphere you begin to recognize them real quick. It's really amazing to me where goodness likes to show up. This might surprise you. It turns out that goodness tends to thrive in a mess. If you've got a terrible mess, it's a perfect incubator for God's *goodness* to thrive. Goodness will always oppose evil, and evil is overcome by goodness because goodness wants to advance. Goodness doesn't tolerate evil and evil moves to the back burner when goodness shows up. This ongoing event tends to be startling.

Light is superior to darkness and *goodness* is far superior to evil. So goodness shows up and tears darkness apart and it tends to be messy. Even impolite.

> *And God saw the light, that it was good:*
> *and God divided the light from the darkness.*
>
> –Genesis 1:4 KJV

God loves to be in the addition and in the multiplication business. But when it comes to confronting evil and darkness, He drops His supernatural math into the division business.

Because light is superior to darkness in every way and *goodness* is superior to evil in every way, God just decided to move the darkness out of the way and displace it with the goodness of light.

Boom!

With the goodness package comes lots of confidence and courage because goodness is right. Goodness needs to be there and evil does not. It really is that simple.

Consequently, there is a lot of confrontation with goodness. There tends to be a lot of yelling and slanderous accusations thrown at goodness. Sparks fly when goodness shows up. Division tends to be messy.

THE GOOD GUYS

Some of my favorite historical heroes are warriors who stood up against the momentum and rising surge of the evil of their day. I want to stand with those guys and I want to be deeply connected to a kingdom tribe who do the same.

I want to shoot cover for Davy Crocket swinging his empty barreled musket and screaming from the adobe walls of the Alamo. I want to help William Wallace defy the King Longshanks and actually dare to invade England. I want to support Wellington while he was chasing down the tyrant Napoleon. I love it when the good guys confront the bad guys and it's not in places of safety where this happens. I want to be there with Elliot Ness when he was pointing at the bully Al Capone and proclaiming, "I am untouchable!" I want to shake Frank Hammer's hand for coming out of retirement to end the murderous exploits of Bonnie and Clyde with a double barreled shot gun. I want to ride with Houston over the rise on the fields of San Jacinto strait towards the tent of the dictator Santa Anna.

There is actually a GLORY to the confrontation against evil, a dangerous glory.

Warriors have always sniffed the winds of glory on the holy grounds of terrible confrontation and conflict. Can you see it in tiny Miss Rosa Parks? So you shouldn't be surprised that we tend to find glorious goodness in messy, even dark and scary places. Let's unpack this.

GOD'S DECLARATION OF WAR IS CALLED GOODNESS

The first time we see Goodness is in the creation story that Moses wrote down for us. At the end of every day, in the midst of darkness, God said it was good. While everything was messy, unfinished, and in a state of deformed transition, while stars exploded and gamma rays shot through the heavens, while nothing was as it should be and everything was still unfinished, God declared His *goodness* right there.

> *. . .and God saw that it was good.*
>
> –Genesis 1:25 KJV

The Lord waged war against the disorder, darkness, and chaos by seeing to it and proclaiming and demonstrating His *goodness*. This is how He changes atmospheres, by introducing goodness. We should do the same.

> *And we know that for those who love God*
> *all things work together for good,*
> *for those who are called according to his purpose.*
>
> –Romans 8:28 ESV

We are not afraid of the mess because since we love God, the mess becomes employed by the *goodness* of God. The Bible says here that our love for God qualifies us to see all things work together for GOOD. Goodness is God's ongoing work for those who love Him and are called according to His purpose.

Let me tell you that there is a lot of warfare involved in that work. If you and I are partnering with Him in this earth, we will not be in clean, pristine, and sterile environments. We will be in prisons bringing the gospel. We will be among our poorest, feeding and helping them. We will be in trash dumps throughout the world with clean clothes and water. We will be in brothels and cat houses delivering young girls from the horrors of sex trafficking.

We are not afraid of the darkness because it is inferior to the light within us. The work of light and goodness is always in the midst of a huge mess, at first. But here's the good news. Christ is in the midst of us.

> *For where two or three are gathered*
> *together in my name, there am I in the midst of them.*
>
> –Matthew 18:20 KJV

> *And ye shall know that I am in the midst of Israel,*
> *and that I am the LORD your God, and none else: and my people shall never be ashamed.*
>
> –Joel 2:27 KJV

> *For I, saith the LORD,*
> *will be unto her a wall of fire round about,*
> *and will be the glory in the midst of her.*
>
> –Zechariah 2:5 KJV

So there He is in the midst of this terrible mess called you and I, and there we go as His people into the messes of this world with the mandate and mission to change things.

We are surrounded by his *goodness,* first He leads us by it.

> *Teach me to do thy will; for thou art my God:*
> *thy spirit is good; lead me*
> *into the land of uprightness.*
>
> –Psalm 143:10 KJV

Then after He leads us by His *goodness,* we are followed by His *goodness.*

> *Surely goodness and mercy shall follow me*
> *all the days of my life,*
> *and I shall dwell in the house of the Lord forever.*
>
> –Psalm 23:6

So not only is He in the midst of us with His goodness but He is before us and behind us with His goodness.

> *Then your light will break forth like the dawn, and your healing will quickly appear; then your righteousness will go before you, and the glory of the LORD will be your rear guard.*
>
> –Isaiah 58:8 NIV

So it's from the sanctuary of goodness, in the midst of terrible messes, the kingdom is born in the earth.

God is not afraid of our mess. Determine right now to run to God with your messes instead of running away from Him because of them. When we no longer run from God but run to God with our messes, we eventually learn to not run from evil and the messes of this world because *good* overcomes evil. That's when the church starts taking on hell with a water pistol.

THE EXPERIENCE OF GOODNESS AND THE FINE WINE OF HIS PRESENCE

It turns out that what happens in the mess and the hurt, through all the discomfort and the ongoing, unfinished business of dreams yet unfulfilled, is that we personally experience His goodness. It's not something we read about or even hope for, but it is something we actually personally experience.

Check out this amazing verse of scripture:

> *O taste and see that the LORD is good;*
> *Blessed is the man who takes refuge in Him!*
>
> –Psalm 34:8 ESV

So you see, when evil comes against us and we have to take refuge, the blessing is that we taste the *goodness* of God. This is not naturally speaking, it is practically speaking. God equipped us with five major natural senses and now science is saying there are at least nine senses and most researchers think there are more like twenty-one or so.

CLEAR DEFINITION

Just for reference, the commonly held definition of a "sense" is, "Any system that consists of a group of sensory cell types that respond to a specific physical phenomenon and that corresponds to a particular group of regions within the brain where the signals are received and interpreted."

There are other senses previously not recognized, like our ability to perceive time or pressure, or tension or when someone walks in the room without us seeing them or hearing them. All of these are natural representations of how we perceive things spiritually.

Let's talk supernatural senses for a minute. We will stick with the common five and look at their supernatural counterpart. We will get to what it means to taste.

***1. Seeing* represents perception through supernatural vision._**

These guys get it._Prophetic conceptual ideas and long term plans belong to seers. Seers are visionary dreamers and tend to be outcome based and goal oriented. Anything visual is a big deal to people who are seers. Maps, timelines, geography, patterns, and models speak in a huge way to seers. Seeing is connected to big picture kingdom thinking.
They tend to be very intentional and the completion of certain tasks is very important to them. Because they see what others do not, they tend to be lonely and misunderstood, and because of that their skill sets are far less social and much more administrative. Seers are navigational creatures and develop into CEO types.

> *Formerly in Israel, when a man went to inquire of God, he would say, 'Come, let us go to the seer,' because the prophet of today used to be called a seer.*
> –I Samuel 9:9 NIV

Seers tend to see visions, dreams, and circumstances. Don't let this freak you out. This is normal for kingdom people. We "see" in the spirit in a number of different ways. Dreams are moving and dynamic while we are asleep. Visions are moving and dynamic while we are awake. Pictures are static, just one image or scene, which I call Holy Ghost flashcards. It's a normal part of kingdom living to see things prophetically while sleeping or while wide awake. Check out just a few biblical examples:

And he [Jacob] came to a certain place and stayed there that night, because the sun had set. Taking one of the stones of the place, he put it under his head and lay down in that place to sleep. [12]*And he dreamed, and behold, there was a ladder set up on the earth, and the top of it reached to heaven. And behold, the angels of God were ascending and descending on it!*

–Genesis 28:11-12 ESV

And having been warned in a dream not to return to Herod, they [the Magi] left for their own country by another road.

–Matthew 2:12 NRSV

After these things the word of the Lord came to Abram in a vision, "Do not be afraid, Abram, I am your shield; your reward shall be very great."

–Genesis 15:1 NRSV

One afternoon about three o'clock he [Cornelius] had a vision in which he clearly saw an angel of God coming in and saying to him, "Cornelius."

–Acts 10:3 NRSV

This is what the Lord showed me... a basket of summer fruit.

–Amos 8:1 ESV

"Look," he [Stephen] said, "I see heaven opened and the son of man standing at the right hand of God!"

–Acts 7:56 ESV

The beginning of things and the pioneering of new moves of God tend to belong to the seers among us.

2. *Hearing* represents perception through knowing what God is supernaturally saying.

Communication tends to belong to the realm of hearers. Hearers bring clear definition and language to invisible things. I love hearers. Hearing is definitely about the social and horizontal end of the prophetic realm. We need skilled articulates who know what to do and how to communicate it. God bless the hearers among us.

One of the greatest communicators ever, a brother by the name of Paul, the biggest writer of the New Testament, was an awesome hearer.

> *He fell to the ground and heard a voice saying to him...*
>
> –Acts 9:4 NIV

> *While they were worshipping the Lord and fasting, the Holy Spirit said, Set apart for me Barnabas and Saul...*
>
> –Acts 13:2 ESV

> *And a vision appeared to Paul in the night. A man of Macedonia stood and pleaded with him, saying, "Come over to Macedonia and help us."*
>
> –Acts 16:9

> *One night the Lord said to Paul in a vision, "Do not be afraid, but speak and do not be silent..."*
>
> –Acts 18:9 NRSV

> *Now, after these things had been accomplished, Paul resolved in the Spirit to go through Macedonia and Achaia, and then go on to Jerusalem.*
>
> –Acts 19:21 NRSV

> *That night the Lord stood near him and said, "Keep up your courage! For just as you have testified for me in Jerusalem, so you must bear witness also in Rome."*
>
> –Acts 23:11 NRSV

With hearing comes all kinds of ways to skillfully and creatively communicate the heart of God. As hearers develop their skill sets in knowing the heart of God, they also develop in communication.

3. *Smelling* represents supernatural discernment.

People who perceive really deeply and have a gift for identification tend to be supernatural sniffers. They come with what I call a Holy Ghost BS detector. Yes, I just said that. You've been grown up long enough to handle such cultural verbiage. People with the nose of the Holy Ghost tend to be atmosphere and environment stewards. I like that.

4. ***Feelings*** **represents perception through supernatural and holy emotions.**

I think these people tend to be more about the heart of God. Feelers tend to be more dramatic and more passionate or more broken than they are communicators. A great cross prophetic gift to me, would be feelers and hearers but I haven't seen a lot of that especially in the first years of being saved. Feelers tend to have physical sensations.

> *My heart throbs like a harp for Moab, and my very soul for Kir-heres.*
>
> –Isaiah 16:11 NRSV

> *My anguish, my anguish! I writhe in pain!*
>
> –Jeremiah 4:19 NRSV

God may speak to these guys using impressions. They sense something deep within and know that it's God speaking to them or showing them something. It may be in the sensing of great joy, deep sorrow, compassion, strength, or something like that. Even pain may indicate something that they need to pray about.

> *When he [Jesus] saw the crowds he had great compassion for them, because they were harassed and helpless like sheep without a shepherd.*
>
> –Matthew 9:36 NRSV

> *For I [Paul] wrote you out of much distress and anguish of heart and with many tears, not to cause you pain, but to let you know the abundant love that I have for you.*
>
> –2 Corinthians 2:4 NRSV

5. But ***tasting,*** **ah, tasting is all about supernatural, personal experience and personal, unique encounter._**

Tasters are people who first know to note the circumstances in which God showed up in such an awesome encounter and they appreciate it. There are certain people and certain atmospheres where you can TASTE God in a radical way. Others you can't. Tasters learn to set environments and make a big deal out of setting them. This is part of the romance of personal, intimate experience.

You either get it, or you don't.

In the natural our taste buds detect sweet, sour, salty, and bitter. All of these are representative of personal experience with Christ.

- Sweet has to do with the things that are so pleasing to all of us. It's the part of the Holy Spirit that we really appreciate and hope for.
- Sour is obviously important to taste and has to do with strong experiences that are not easy to take in or digest. They don't have to all be bad because a lot of sour is actually good, but you have to develop a taste for sour. Babies can't handle sour because it's just too strong. There is a way you can experience God at a mature level that you certainly can not at an immature level.
- Saltiness is all about enhancement of flavor. I think that there is a way you can experience the Lord that leaves you way more thirsty than before you experienced Him. Salt tends to do that. There are personal encounters that greatly intensify your other encounters and leave you thirsty for much, much more.
- Bitterness is a legitimate part of our experience with God.

> *And I went unto the angel, and said unto him, Give me the little book. And he said unto me, Take it, and eat it up; and it shall make thy belly bitter, but it shall be in thy mouth sweet as honey.*
>
> –Revelation 10:9 KJV

Remember that tasting is personal experience. The word, heart of God, or how we know Jesus starts off as sweet but brings us to a bitter place. What the heck is that?

It's the Lord leading us and directing us into places that would never otherwise set well with us. He doesn't tell us everything up front and once we encounter Him we become committed to something we never would have committed to other wise.

It's bittersweet. That means it's something wonderful that we had to pay a big price for. Jesus perfectly explained this process to Peter like this:

> *"Very truly I tell you, when you were younger you dressed yourself and went where you wanted; but when you are old you will stretch out your hands, and someone else will dress you and lead you where you do not want to go."*
>
> –John 21:18 NIV

The bitter part of experiencing Jesus is the part where we go where we never would have gone without Him.

THE TASTE OF WATER INTO WINE

When it comes to tasting wine, I am some what of a Holy Ghost wino.

I think that wine is a huge counterpart to something very supernatural in the kingdom. Let's talk about tasting wine.

The simplest flavors to recognize are so easy. Very ripe, jammy fruit, and strong vanilla flavors from various oak treatments taste something like soft drinks. It is perfectly natural for new wine drinkers to relate to them first, because they are familiar and likable. Some extremely successful wine brands have been formulated to offer these flavors in abundance. But they do not offer complexity and that's the way it is with tasting or experiencing God's presence. He shows up first in ways that you can easily recognize, but then He moves you onto much more unique and complex *tasting* or experiences with Him. That's called fine wine.

> *On this mountain the Lord Almighty will prepare a*
> *feast of rich food for all peoples,*
> *a banquet of aged wine—*
> *the best of meats and the finest of wines.*
>
> –Isaiah 25:6 NIV

Complex and fine wines seem to dance in your mouth. They change, even as you're tasting them. They are like good paintings, the more you look at them the more there is to see. In older wines, these complexities sometimes evolve into the realm of the sublime. The length of a wine, whether old or young, is one good indication of complexity. All you have to do is note how long the flavors linger after you swallow. Most beginning wine drinkers move on too quickly to the next sip when a really good wine is in the glass. Hold on! Just like that, most Christians are into Boone's Farm when they ought to be into something way,

way past that. Let the wine finish its dance before you change partners and the Lord continue His experience with you before you go onto a new encounter.

A complete wine is balanced, harmonious, complex, and evolves with a lingering, satisfying finish. Such wines deserve extra attention, because they have more to offer and so do such Christians.

We need to learn to truly savor God's *goodness* and not just swallow for the sake of digesting. It's from learning and appreciating our complex experience with God that we learn to know God's *goodness*. Let's look at that verse one more time:

> *O taste and see that the LORD is good;*
> *How blessed is the man who takes refuge in Him!*
>
> –Psalm 34:8 NASB

Not, "O *consume* and see that the Lord is good," but *taste!* Let God show you His goodness through a lingering and on going personal experience with Him. Kingdom learning is not cerebral. How we learn Jesus is not through books and teaching alone. We learn Him through how we have personally tasted His goodness, savored it and thought about it after the experience with Him is long gone. Tasting is personal experience, and mature tasting involves exploring and identifying the complexities and layers it has to offer.

God's *goodness* is like that.

I think a lot of God's goodness skips off of us the way a meteor deflects off of our atmosphere. We go onto the next thing without any kind of dedication to contemplation or meditation. Instead of thinking God thoughts we worry and swat at anxiety with all our mental muscles.

But sometimes the gravity pull of our broken hearts will bring in God's *goodness* in a way that lights up the sky and comes screaming in. When that happens, the impact is thunderous and completely alters the geography of our lives.

THE OUTCOME OF GOODNESS IS TRANSFORMATION

Transformation begins at goodness. Goodness is the very first step of total transformation.

Do you remember that I told you how Goodness shows up in a mess? The deal is, once Goodness is engaged the mess is no longer the issue because Goodness always takes center stage.

God's *goodness* is a thermostat and not a thermometer. It changes the tone and resets the atmosphere. Goodness changes things permanently. That's why at the beginning of the creation story and at the end of every day God said, "It is good." Goodness is the catalyst of transition.

RENT TO OWN BLUES

Nearly thirty years ago I took a job working for a rent to own company and a big part of my responsibilities was to be the repo man in six different housing projects in Ft. Worth, Texas.
Even though I had been called every racial and hateful name you can imagine, even though I had personally removed TVs, refrigerators, and all kinds of appliances out of peoples homes, we saw a tremendous revival in those dark and desperate places. Leanna and I did a kids crusade and in one single day we baptized over 100 people in the same place where people had thrown bottles at me and cussed me like a dog.

Goodness is what changed everything.

Because Leanna and I started a ministry where we bought refurbished refrigerators, washers and dryers, and cooking stoves. Every time I would repo one in the name of my company, I would return later that evening in the name of Jesus with a running one that was paid for and just give it to them. The same people that had threatened my life earlier would weep and apologize. They would also attend bible studies and send their kids to our outreaches.

...the goodness of God leads you to repentance

–Romans 2:4

Good and upright is the LORD:
Therefore will He teach sinners in the way

–Psalm 25:8

Goodness always teaches us something true about God. The outcome of goodness is transformation because goodness says things need to change for the better.

GOOD OVERCOMES EVIL.

"How did Jesus expect His disciples to react under persecution? (In Matthew 5:12 He said), 'Rejoice and be glad!' We are not to retaliate like an unbeliever, nor sulk like a child, nor lick our wound in self-pity like a dog, nor just grin and bear it like a Stoic, still less pretend we enjoy it like a masochist. What then? We are to rejoice as a Christian should and even 'leap for joy' (Lk. 6:23)."

–John Stott

CHAPTER 8

THE FINAL CHAPTER

Overcoming the persecution and rejection of Goodness in these last days

This last chapter comes with lots of warnings and sobering insight to the importance of loving *good,* even when it's painful. I will close on practical ideas of injecting God's goodness into a realm that is opposed to it.

Let's get brave.

> *"... who is he who will harm you if you become followers of what is good? But even if you should suffer for righteousness' sake, you are blessed. And do not be afraid of their threats, nor be troubled. But sanctify the Lord God in your hearts, and always be ready to give a defense to everyone who asks you a reason for the hope that is in you, with meekness and fear; having a good conscience, that when they defame you as evildoers, those who revile your good conduct in Christ may be ashamed."*
>
> –I Peter 3:13-16

Persecution is coming in America against those of us who follow good and demonstrate God's *goodness.* Notice I didn't say persecution is coming *to* America. Because it is coming *from* America and against its own Christian citizens. We are being called evil doers when, in fact, we are not. The point, as illustrated in this scripture, is to "defame" us or try and remove any influence we have over the culture. Hey, this is part of the program and I want to map it out for you. It's not a fun part but it is a necessary part because it keeps us separate from the world and firmly planted as the good guys. Don't forget that good guys are warriors.

We are close to the return of Jesus. As we get closer and closer people will be deceived and a big part of that deception is that the world will call good evil and evil will be called good. That means the good guys become outcasts and this happens when a society doesn't have a value for truth. That means not only will the world not celebrate good but the world will hate good and love evil. The world will celebrate evil and become antagonistic against good and it gets exponential.

We are already living in that day and the heat is about to be turned up. Lock and load your spiritual weapons of warfare.

SYMPATHY FOR THE DEVIL

Back in 1968, when the Rolling Stones released their new album, *Beggars Banquet,* the opening track captured the world's attention. *Sympathy for the Devil,* a rock song with a latin rhythm, would be a big hit. *Rolling Stone Magazine* would later list it as #32 on the list of 500 greatest songs of all time. I personally think it was part of a prophetic voice for the times-that-were-a-changing. A time, the last times, where the devil starts to become the world's hero.

BLASPHEMOUS TITLES

Just two years later, a leather-bound coptic language papyrus document found in Egypt would make world news. Self titled, "The Gospel of Judas" (Euangelion Ioudas), it was an ancient writing which relates the story of Jesus's death from the viewpoint of Judas as the good guy. Of course Jesus is the bad guy and the whole thing was a set up for poor Judas.

> *"You love evil more than good...."*
>
> –Psalm 52:3

If you jump from books to modern movies, God is increasingly portrayed as the bad guy. In 2014, we couldn't wait for *Noah,* directed by visionary filmmaker Darren Aronofsky. Guess what we were treated to? God is the bad guy who refuses to speak to people who desperately need Him and fallen angels, demons, the Bible calls them, were the good guys as some kind of weird, selfless bunch of rock monsters. Whatever Noah was, he was not the first left winged treehugger and ultra environmentalist. Maybe it was that kind of talk that drove the brother to drinking.

Millions of people all over the world now know this modern fable as the story of Noah's Ark.

> *For the time will come when*
> *they will not endure sound doctrine...*
> *and they will turn their ears away from the truth, and be turned aside to fables.*
>
> –2 Timothy 4:3-4

But I had a lot bigger hope for Ridley Scott's version of the *Exodus*. The Story of God's great deliverance of the Jews from Egypt's slavery is so well known, and Ridley Scott is such a great director. *White Squall, Alien, Gladiator,* and *Kingdom of Heaven* are four of my top twenty favorite movies. Oh, I couldn't wait!

But these are the days when *good* is called evil. Pharaoh was the good guy and fell victim to God as a fit throwing child. Wow!

It's as they say in the 2014 movie *The Maze Runner,* "Wicked is good."

> *"But he who sins against me wrongs his own soul;*
> *All those who hate me love death."*
>
> –Proverbs 8:36

HOLY GHOST ROCKSTARS

What is celebrated in heaven is not celebrated on the earth because the King of heaven is not celebrated on this earth. Jesus is the ruler of things in heaven and my friend, He is good.

> *And Jesus said unto him,*
> *Why call me good? None is good, except one,*
> *that is, God*
>
> –Luke 18:19

The One that is good is coming back soon and as there is more and more opposition to His appearance, there will be a greater hostility against the appearance of His *goodness*.

It doesn't matter. We fight to hold on to goodness.

GOODNESS AND TRUTH ARE BOTH SOMETHING YOU HAVE TO HOLD ON TO

You better hold on and test the truthful metal of everything. In these days, you will be challenged to believe life is life and death is death. You will be tempted like no other generation to give up on goodness. Throw out the supernatural bastard of evil and hold onto to the legitimate sonship of the *goodness* of Jesus Christ.

> *But test everything; hold fast what is good.*
>
> –I Thessalonians 5:21 ESV

> *Let love be genuine.*
> *Abhor what is evil; hold fast to what is good.*
>
> –Romans 12:9 ESV

Do you see the common biblical theme of loving good goes hand in hand with loving truth? If you do not hold onto what is true and what is genuine, you will not hold onto what is good. You will let it go for your own selfish and destructive ambitions. Truth and goodness are so attached, we are commanded to think about both in Philippians 4:8:

> *Finally, brethren, whatever things are true, whatever things are noble, whatever things are just, whatever things are pure, whatever things are lovely, whatever things are of good report, if there is any virtue and if there is anything praiseworthy—meditate on these things.*
>
> –Philippians 4:8

STRANGER DANGER

Some of the biggest warnings that come from the Bible tell us to be super careful that we don't call evil good and good evil. The Lord has a holy hatred for the portrayal of His glory as something shameful.

"How long, O you sons of men,
will you turn my glory to shame?
How long will you love ***worthlessness***
and seek falsehood?"

–Psalm 4:2-3 (emphasis mine)

You don't call worthless things glorious and shameful things wonderful without God saying, "Really?" If you have no value for what's real you lose your value for what's good.

DRAMA QUEEN

In the year 2015, the pop culture world was rocked by the man formally known as Bruce Jenner and his sexy pose on the front cover of *Vanity Fair Magazine.* The sixty-five-year-old grandfather sprawled out in Hollywood glamour as an ultra airbrushed beauty in none other than an Annie Leibovitz photograph. Sporting new perfect breasts and a beautiful face that had recently been feminized through reconstructive surgery, he leaned back in a beautiful woman's form with the words, "Call me Caitlyn" written across the page.

If you have a heart for truth and a prophetic eye to see, you can see how Jenner is a willing puppet of something he knows nothing about. Bruce Jenner is not the enemy. He's just a guy, or a girl, depending upon your point of view, that is trying to find peace and happiness. He even said that this is way bigger than him and in that, he was right. The spirit behind him is a dark demonic movement and is something destructive to human beings and any form of civilized society where goodness abounds.

The name Caitlyn means "purity" and in this generation what is nasty will be demanded to be called pure. What is drama will actually be called reality. You don't have to hate Bruce Jenner. He has every right to manipulate his body however he wants to, but you don't have to call evil good either.

Woe to those who call evil good, and good evil;
Who put darkness for light, and light for darkness....

–Isaiah 5:20

In the subsequent and beautifully written column by Buzz Bissenger, Bruce Jenner says that as Bruce, he was always telling lies, but that as Caitlyn Jenner, she doesn't have any lies. Mind you, he says this while doing his best to keep his male genitalia from spilling out of a form-fitting satin corset, and nobody questions it! Nobody points out how ridiculous the whole notion of such a thing is because selfish drama is celebrated as courageous reality in American pop culture.

There are no lies with what he says as long as you change the meaning of the word "truth" and the meaning of the word "lie" and simply reverse them. The book of Romans tells us about those people and apparently Paul was talking about us.

> *Who changed the truth of God into a lie,*
> *and worshipped and served the creature*
> *more than the Creator.*
>
> –Romans 1:25 KJV

Today, anything dramatic that makes you feel good through selfish ambition is called good and will be celebrated even if it is destructive. But it's not celebrated in heaven. It's not called purity in heaven.

While I do not find it attractive, I am not bothered by his lifestyle or his decisions with what he does with his own body. He will stand before God and answer for that on his own, I have nothing to say about it and really, it's none of my business. I feel no need to protest him or be mean to him in any way. He's an olympian athlete and could probably kick my butt. It would be super embarrassing to be manhandled by an old lady. I would have no reason to be anything other than respectful and nice to him if I saw him.

However, I object to the evil of the mandate that comes from our society and from the headlines on our media that demand I call his lifestyle pure. God demands I do the opposite. I would much rather be on God's side than on the wand of *Harry Potter* (Hollywood).

VANITY FAIR

The title of the magazine Jenner emerges as a woman on, paints an even bigger picture and is the most prophetic of all. All of this is under the title of a circus of worthlessness: *Vanity Fair.*

I hear God asking America a question from the book of Psalm:

> *"How long will you love* ***worthlessness*** *and seek falsehood?"*
>
> –Psalm 4:2 (emphasis mine)

The word "vanity" means worthless and the Bible says, while the world would say different, there is no real value in all these things celebrated today.

When I think of Bruce Jenner on the cover of *Vanity Fair,* demanding our generation to call him a name that means "pure" and to say he is a woman, I think of Psalm 119:37:

> *Turn away mine eyes from beholding vanity: and quicken thou me in thy way.*
>
> –Psalm 119:37 KJV

> *Turn away my eyes from looking at worthless things, And revive me in Your ways.*
>
> –Psalm 119:37

> *Let my eyes be turned away from what is false; give me life in your ways.*
>
> –Psalm 119:37 BBE

WHEN GOODNESS IS NOT CELEBRATED BUT VANITY IS, IT MOVES US INTO PLACES OF DRAUGHT AND JUDGMENT

> *"...you have polluted the land with your harlotries and your wickedness. Therefore the showers have been withheld, and there has been no latter rain. You have had a harlot's forehead; You refuse to be ashamed."*
>
> –Jeremiah 3:2-3

I think it's amazing to consider that at the time, the very next month after *Vanity Fair Magazine* came out with Bruce Jenner as Caitlyn, it was announced by *Scientific American Magazine* that California was suffering the greatest draught in recorded history.

THE BREAKFAST OF CHAMPIONS

In an article by Dan Baum, he starts off his incredible story by talking about one of my ancestors, William Brewer, who first set out to conduct the very first geological survey of California in 1860. While Brewer was stomping around in California, his cousins and my great great grandfathers were fighting for Texas in the Civil War and were busy about the business of horrible destruction that would last for generations. This could get me shot in Texas for saying this but they should've gone with him.

Anyway, *Scientific American* said, "The drought is transforming California in almost every conceivable way: meteorologically, geologically, biologically, agriculturally, socially, economically, and politically."

Yeah, when you pollute the land with harlotries and refuse to be ashamed of it, it brings a game changing draught that even science magazines will report.

KINGDOM PREPPING

So here is your overcomers kit for getting through the days that are coming, and it all has to do with *truth* and *goodness*.

1. LOVE GOOD AND HATE EVIL

Love what is good. Do good. Celebrate anything that is selfless and good. Have a huge value for the betterment of other people and remember that good overcomes evil. Have the kingdom's perspective of selfless giving and transformation as good. Do whatever you can to bring the geography of heaven into this earth. Live as a redeemed community in the midst of an ungodly society. Love what God loves and hate what God hates.

> *Let love be without hypocrisy. Abhor what is evil. Cling to what is good. [10]Be kindly affectionate to one another with brotherly love, in honor giving preference to one another; [11]not lagging in diligence, fervent in spirit, serving the Lord; [12]rejoicing in hope, patient in tribulation, continuing steadfastly in prayer; [13]distributing to the needs of the saints, given to hospitality.*
>
> –Romans 12:9-13

- Search after and fall in love with God's heart.
- Demonstrate God's heart and attitude towards other people.
- Keep yourself passionate about what God is passionate about.

2. INFLUENCE EVERYTHING WITH GOD'S GOODNESS

Post and publish any good things you see or know about. Be a thermostat and not a thermometer. Set a different tone with goodness and have a different word of hope. Live according to a different spirit than the rest of the world and know that good overcomes evil.

> *In the beginning was the Word, and the Word was with God, and the Word was God. [2]He was in the beginning with God. [3]All things were made through Him, and without Him nothing was made that was made. [4]In Him was life, and the life was the light of men. [5]And the light shines in the darkness, and the darkness did not comprehend it.*
>
> –John 1:1-5

- Don't be famous for who you stand against, be known for how you stand with Jesus.
- Be known for what you do, not what you don't do. Make sure it is good.

- Make it your purpose to make God's *goodness* known.

3. DEVELOP SELFLESS KINGDOM SKILL SETS AND GIFTS OF GOODNESS

Do not guard your heart, but let yourself get wrecked with the pain of others. Lack of empathy is the essence of all evil. Make yourself consider the plights and the hurts of struggling lives in your world. Submerge yourself in those worlds knowing that Christ is in the midst of you. Get skilled at the culture and bring in an entirely different spirit. Let Goodness lead you into the messy places that beg for the good guys to show up, and when you get there keep doing things until you are doing goodness right.

> *"Behold, I send you out as sheep in the midst of wolves. Therefore be wise as serpents and harmless as doves."*
>
> –Matthew 10:16

- Don't just support ministries that are involved, get personally involved.
- Feed people, clothe people, visit the hurting and the lonely, and give generously.
- Find creative and fresh ways to make people's lives better, cleaner, healthier, more fun, more colorful, and at a higher quality.

4. WHEN YOU DO SOMETHING IN THE NAME OF JESUS, LET GOODNESS BE THE FACE WITH THE NAME

Don't just teach Jesus, teach the *goodness* of Jesus through selfless acts of service and demonstrations of what heaven values. If you feed people, treat them with honor and dignity and give better food than they expect. Give more food than they thought and tell them thank you for coming. Dress your best and treat them as if they paid $200 to be at your food bank. Go out of your way to make them comfortable and go after supernatural healing and powerful miracles knowing that power and authority come in the context of service and knowing that goodness overcomes evil.

> *And my speech and my preaching was not with enticing words of man's wisdom, but in demonstration of the Spirit and of power*
>
> –I Corinthians 2:4 KJV

- Jesus has preferences and His should be ours when we do good.
- Jesus has a personality and His should flavor all of our goodness.
- How people are treated in heaven should be how people are treated on this earth when we are doing good.

5. LET GOOD ALWAYS BE A CATALYST FOR KINGDOM TRANSFORMATION

Take action. Take decisive action. Do things that matter. When you do something good make it sustainable and do it with excellence. Remain faithful and committed to working towards real, tangible change. Develop and empower others to carry on where you cannot. Make a difference and make it way bigger than you.

> [7]*Do not be deceived, God is not mocked; for whatever a man sows, that he will also reap.* [8]*For he who sows to his flesh will of the flesh reap corruption, but he who sows to the Spirit will of the Spirit reap everlasting life.* [9]*And let us not grow weary while doing good, for in due season we shall reap if we do not lose heart.* [10]*Therefore, as we have opportunity, let us do good to all, especially to those who are of the household of faith*
>
> –Galatians 6:7-10

- We live in a constant awareness that nothing is impossible and God's *goodness* makes true transformation a real possibility anywhere.
- We live to see His will done on earth as it is in heaven and what's not in heaven shouldn't be here. What is in heaven should be here. Where it is not like that, we change it and it always starts with goodness.
- Since there is no end concerning His kingdom and of his peace, as the Bible says, there is no end to how things can change for the better. In the small time we have on this earth, we will make changes that far outlast all of us and glorify the King.

GOOD OVERCOMES EVIL.

CONCLUSION

So I wrap up this book. This is my eighth published book and I always feel a lot of joy in accomplishing my fuzzy visions of what a book can be. I especially feel joy now. It's my seventh night of vacation on a remote island in the Caribbean called Curasau. I sit in room 435 at the Renaissance Hotel, looking out at the ocean, the sun setting as I type.

All I can say as I sit in this blessed place, is God is *good*. The great bigness of this goodness so diminishes the evil I have experienced in the past. As you have read, goodness does that.

I close by saying thank you for reading and thank you for your fight for goodness.

My brilliant and smoking hot, *good* wife of twenty-six years showed me the very end of the book of Nehemiah today, and I would like to steal his line for a fitting finish.

I close by saying to the King of Kings what the great ancient rebuilder of Jerusalem said when he ended his book:

> ...***Remember me, O my God, for good!***
>
> –Nehemiah 13:31 (emphasis mine)

ABOUT THE AUTHOR

Troy Allen Brewer can't spell, type or mark a legible letter but he never let it keep him from being a writer. His elementary school years were full of fantasy novels with his friends as the characters. When they made him mad, dragons would eat them or their space ship would suddenly crash through a worm hole.

He still writes today and his "Fresh from the Brewer" newspaper columns are read by tens of thousands of beloved readers every week. His sermons are heard by the congregation he pastors and people throughout the world. So as long as close friends are willing to edit his chicken scratch, write he will.

Born and raised in the same area of North Texas, he still calls the city of Joshua "home."

His four kids still call him "Dad," and Leanna, his bride of 26 years, still calls him hers.

Troy's high school years were spent playing guitar, riding bulls, dodging work and even making moonshine.

In May of 1986, at the age of 19, he received Christ and fully dedicated his life to the kingdom and ministry. He married Leanna three years later and they spent the first few years of their marriage involved in music and youth ministry.

In 1995, after falling in love with feeding the poor, he and his wife founded a church called Open Door Ministries. Today, OpenDoor Church is an amazing congregation of extraordinary people that give away more than four million pounds of food every year to the needy of Johnson County. Their food bank warehouse blesses as many as fifty thousand people annually with food and care items.

Troy's nationally broadcast radio program, *Experiencing Real Life,* is heard everyday throughout the United States.

Today Troy teaches regularly at OpenDoor Church and speaks at conferences and events throughout the world. He has made more than 100 mission trips in at least 39 different nations covering every continent on the globe.

You can contact him at 817-295-7671 or at
PO Box 1349 Joshua, Texas 76058

You can also visit Troy and tour his work at:
www.TroyBrewer.com or
www.OpenDoorExperience.com

OTHER BOOKS BY TROY A. BREWER

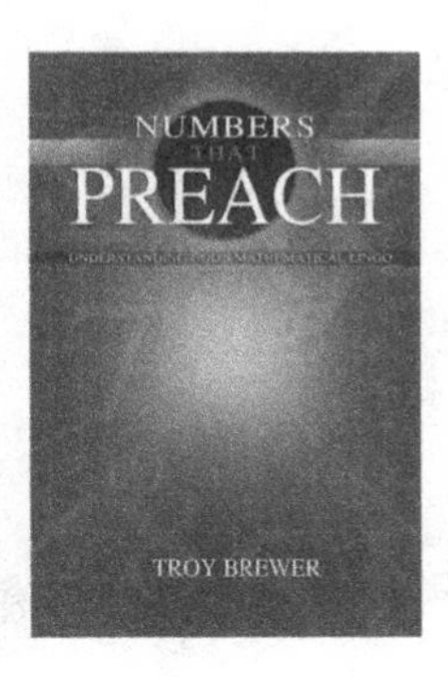

Numbers That Preach
Hidden sermons that God declares through His mathematical lingo.

Soul Invasion
Biblical strategies for victorious thinking.

Living Life/Forward
Troy skillfully takes you step by step and from faith to faith into unclaimed upgrade.

Miracles with a Message
Things Troy learned from seeing God's miraculous power.

Fresh from the Brewer
Sips of wisdom from The Carpenter's Cup.

Fresh from the Brewer, Volume II
Sips of wisdom from The Carpenter's Cup, Volume II.

Best of the Brewer
A collection of Troy's favorite stories that will encourage you, bless you, and challenge you to go deeper.

CPSIA information can be obtained
at www.ICGtesting.com
Printed in the USA
BVHW080811191221
624358BV00005B/334

9 781593 308926